Praise f

"Kristopher Triana pens the most violent, dep...
craft and care of a poet describing a sunset, only the sunset has
been eviscerated, and dismembered, and it is screaming."

—Wrath James White, author of
The Resurrectionist

"Jesus! And I thought I was sick!"

—Edward Lee, author of *Header*

"One of the most exciting and disturbing voices in extreme horror
in quite some time. His stuff hurts so good."

—Brian Keene, author of *Earthworm Gods*

"Having already proved himself a master of extreme horror with
Full Brutal, in *Gone To See The River Man*, Triana shows he is able
to paint his uniquely disturbing visions with a much broader pal-
ette. This gloomily atmospheric novel is an excellent and unnerv-
ing exercise in steadily mounting dread and an inexorable rendez-
vous with doom. It fuses family tragedy with phantasmagoric horror in a way that will linger long in memory. In short, this Triana
guy is a serious contender."

—Bryan Smith, author of *Depraved*

"*Full Brutal* is the most evil thing I have ever read. Each book I
read by this guy only further convinces me that he's one of the
names to watch, an extreme horror superstar in the making."

—Christine Morgan, author of
Lakehouse Infernal

"Whatever style or mode Triana is writing in, the voice matches
it unfailingly."
—*Cemetery Dance*

Blood Relations

Splatterpunk Award-Winning Author
Kristopher Triana

Grindhouse Press
PO BOX 521
Dayton, Ohio 45401

Grindhouse Press #064
ISBN-13: 978-1-941918-61-6

"Dog Years", copyright 2015, first appeared in *Selfies from the End of the World*, an anthology by Mad Scientist Journal.

"The Solution", copyright 2016, first appeared in *Stiff Things*, an anthology by Comet Press.

TABLE OF CONTENTS

for John Wayne Comunale

the brother I never had
until now

"All happy families are alike; each unhappy family is unhappy in its own way."

—Leo Tolstoy, *Anna Karenina*

"You tell me that my brother is my salvation? My salvation? Well then damn him. Damn him in every shape and form and guise. Do I see myself in him? Yes, I do. And what I see sickens me."

—Cormac McCarthy, *The Sunset Limited*

THICKER THAN WATER

WHEN I LOOK THROUGH THE glass separating me from my daughter, I still see traces of her mother in her eyes. The air in the prison is far too close and reeks of exhausted desperation, of bleach and gunmetal. The murmurs all around us create a machine-like thrum. The mood here reminds me of that warm room where quiet piano music played, serenading me as I ran my fingertips over polished oak, comparing the different coffins.

I wonder what Stephanie would think of our Lita now.

"How is your schoolwork going?" I ask.

My daughter's face is pale and distant, a lifeboat lost in a stagnant sea. The harsh fluorescent lights make flares on the lenses of her glasses.

"Fine," she says. "I'm getting good grades."

"That's my girl. What's your favorite subject?"

She shifts, uncomfortable answering even the simplest of questions. She's often twitchy, antsy—just like her mother.

"I don't know," she says, and leaves it at that.

So do I. I know she doesn't like being here.

"Things are going well for me too," I say, "all things considered."

There is a beat. On each side of me are other men, equally hardened by their situations. Privacy partitions divide us, otherwise we are one—a single entity sulking as we speak to our loved ones

1

through phones, even as they sit right in front of us.

"You're getting so tall," I tell her.

She blushes a little and I'm glad to see signs of life. Lita will be fourteen this month. The state forced us apart two years ago, and being without her has dropped me into a bleak and bottomless void. Even these twenty-minute in person visits do little to retract the knife from my heart. If anything, they twist the blade deeper. Watching your daughter grow up in snapshots makes time accelerate. It seems like two weeks ago she still had baby fat in her cheeks and big, curious eyes. Now she has pimples and I can see the cups of a bra beneath her denim shirt. Her hair seems two feet longer than our last visit, and it snakes around her neck in faded ribbons. It stops at her waist now, long and spindly and dirty blond. I wonder if it smells of Stephanie.

"Read anything good lately?" I ask.

She nods. "*The Bell Jar* was good."

I remember having read that in school. It's about a woman with mental illness. This strikes me as an interesting subject for my daughter, but I make no mention of it.

"That's a good one. What else?"

She looks up, searching the ceiling for memories. "*Every Man Dies Alone, Heart of Darkness, Cities of the Plain.*"

"Those are some very adult titles," I say. "But then I guess you're well past Harry Potter now, huh?"

"Yes, Daddy."

Hearing her call me that makes something inside me shatter like a porcelain doll being dropped from a Ferris wheel. Only that summer is long gone now, the carnival closed, and my little girl doesn't play with toys anymore. But I swear I can still smell the funnel cake sometimes, and when I close my eyes at night the lights of the fair are bright and dizzying, parting the soft, brown arms of shadows that try to choke me as I sleep.

A sound alerts us that our time is up and we say a quick goodbye. I touch the glass, wishing it would burst. My body tenses slightly as the guard approaches. These visits go by so quickly. My daughter stands up, her chains jangling at her wrists and ankles, and the guard takes her back into the long, concrete throat of her gray hell.

•••

The house bristles with sunshine and once again I think of hanging curtains on top of the blinds. Slivers of light expose adrift dead skin, revealing an ugliness coating everything like syrup. I try to read a book my daughter is reading, so we'll have more to talk about the next time I see her. She has a lot more time to read than I do, but I'm making an effort to get through at least one chapter before bed each night. During our last phone call, she told me she was reading *Paradise Lost.* The book is lyrical, almost biblical in its flowery prose, and I struggle with it, but understand why it appeals to my daughter. I know how her mind works, how it dissects all that enters it and feeds on the fiery poetry of pain.

I get to speak to her over the phone from the comfort of my home, but the calls are recorded and monitored so we can't talk about what we really want to. I have many questions for her, just as she does for me, but they're private ones—only for the family—so they have to wait.

As the sun falls behind the horizon, the sky turns the same color as the scabs on my knuckles. The yard looks out on a deep canal, but it never rains anymore and the canal is only sugar sand and burnt grass. I smell another wildfire in the distance and hope it spreads into town and devours everyone and everything in its path.

I skip dinner and go upstairs to read my book, hardly processing the words as I touch the empty space on the mattress beside me. Though I lie in bed for twelve hours, I barely sleep at all. When I do, I dream of all the children my wife and I lost before she left me too.

•••

It's my day off and I get up, make coffee but not food, and head into the center of town. Here the sidewalks are brick, and the shops are close together and family owned. This is a sewer for people with disposable income and a false sense of community. Mercifully, it's raining. I hate it here but need to visit the bakeshop. When I step inside, the sugary smell hits me and I flash back to the carnival for a moment, the memory as fresh as if it happened yesterday instead of two years ago.

I hear my wife say, "Can I help you?"

But when I turn around, it isn't her. A heavyset woman with a red atom bomb for hair smiles at me like a department store mannequin. Her apron is pink with smiling puppy faces all over it, her teeth rotted by decades of sweets.

"Oh, hello," I manage. "I'm looking for a birthday cake for my daughter."

3

"How nice," she says. "How old is she going to be?"

"Fourteen."

The woman's head turns to one side, her mouth making an O.

"Teen years," she says. "Look out, Dad!"

She giggles and I force a smile.

"Well," she says, "what does she like?"

"Um, books mostly."

She warthog-snorts a laugh. "I mean what kind of *cake* does she like."

In my pockets, my hands are sweating. I taste copper as I bite the inside of my cheek.

"I don't know," I say.

The woman nods to no one. "Okay. Well, most girls like chocolate. I know I do."

This seems to make perfect sense and I could kiss her for figuring this out for me.

"Chocolate sounds perfect."

"Yes, that's what little girls like."

•••

Visiting days and hours are on a set schedule, so I don't get to see Lita on her actual birthday, but I'm able to see her the day before. It's a special occasion, so we sit at a wooden table together inside the facility with nothing keeping us from each other. Whenever I bring something in, dogs sniff me to check for contraband, but I am allowed to bring in the cake today, as long as it's not in a glass case. We have no knife to cut it, so we put it down between us and pick at it with forks. I don't mind. Knives bring back so many memories, perhaps too many.

"How does it feel to be fourteen?"

She tongues a piece of frosting from the side of her mouth. "The same as thirteen, I guess."

"How's the cake?"

"Good," she says, but I can see her getting twitchy again because of all my questions.

I want to talk to her about *Paradise Lost* but I don't know what to possibly say about the book. Lita looks at me and waits for my eyes to meet hers before speaking.

"I've lived a lot longer than the others, huh, Daddy?"

I swallow, hard and dry. "Yes, honey, you have."

"Sarah only made it to nine, and Tracy only till five and a half."

I nod.

"And Billy died in his crib. How many months was he again?"

"Four."

"He never even got to do anything."

"No," I say, "he didn't."

"At least Tracy got to try. And Sarah did okay, but not like me, right?"

My mind brings up the image of a pale green face bobbing through the algae skin on a pond.

I blink away that summer afternoon and look at my daughter. "Sarah did good, but you know you did better. I'm proud of you, and your mother was too. You know that."

Lita smiles in a way I haven't seen since she was incarcerated. I get the sense she has something going on inside, something she has yet to reveal, but I know better than to ask questions about incomplete work.

"I spoke to the lawyer," I say. "He thinks the psychiatric evaluation can help us out, that we can plead not guilty by reason of insanity."

She shrugs this off as if it doesn't matter, and now I *know* she has something in the works. The prospects of this make my limbs tingle with joy, and I suppress it, reserving myself while I'm still in the prison.

"I'm still being tried as an adult," she reminds me. "They want to make an example out of me."

I hate to admit this truth. "They do."

She stabs her fork into the cake and the raspberry topping oozes out. She plucks the piece of cake free and lets it hover between us like a fat hornet.

"Sarah only killed *one* person," she says, her head held high.

She bites down on the cake and the raspberry filling flows like blood.

•••

Sarah stays on my mind as I drive home.

I was the one to find her and Lindsey. The two of them were best friends, and on that hot afternoon in late August, they were playing down by the pond behind our neighborhood. You could follow the canal in our backyard to it. When the fireflies surfaced, Stephanie called to me from the kitchen, asking if I'd seen the girls. She was preparing dinner, as was Lindsey's mother at her house. It was time for the girls to come home. Leaving my chair, I went outside and the humidity slithered over my skin. I felt like

I was swimming through the air, each breath soggier than the last. The roar of lawnmowers called from the other yards, along with dogs barking at the dying light. Chlorine, charcoal, and cut grass added texture to the air as I walked down the edge of the canal, moving between the dragonflies. When I reached the pond, I called to my daughter, but the only voice that came back to me was my own, echoing off the grove of pines.

I walked along the pond's edge, scanning the surrounding thicket, somehow knowing the girls were nearby. There was a fallen tree that had been on the ground since the hurricane had come a few years prior. Stepping up, I saw the two sets of clothes draped across it—two pairs of short shorts, a pink shirt, and a yellow tank-top. Two sets of flip-flops were on the bank just a few feet away, half sunk in the mud. The girls often wore their swim-suits under their clothes to go swimming when the days got too hot, and today was a scorcher even now that the sun was going down. I held my hand to my forehead as a visor, squinting across the still water flashing pumpkin-colored light into my eyes.

"Sarah? Lindsey?"

I saw a sudden movement but realized it was only the silhou-ettes of ducks. I stepped over the fallen tree, and that's when I saw the first body. It was almost entirely submerged, so I wasn't sure which girl it was at first, but I knew she was dead. I felt suddenly weightless, the world leaving me. Walking into the water, I turned the body over, and little Lindsey gazed up at me with blind eyes. She was already blue, tongue hanging out, the chain still tight around her neck. As she bobbed on the surface, the move-ment dislodged Sarah's body from somewhere below. I saw my daughter's face beneath the lime-colored water. Her smile was wide and glowing even in death, the other end of the chain coiled around her wrists and clenched in her hands. My heart swelled with grief and understanding. There was sorrow here, for certain, but there was no surprise. I'd known it was coming. I had never doubted Sarah would see it through.

Tears came and I sat on the fallen tree for a long time.

When I fell back to earth from wherever I had gone, I came in too fast and felt myself burning. I unwrapped the chain and re-moved it from both girls, then walked deep into the woods, the darkness creeping in, and tossed it into the sorrow of the brush. I went back to the pond, pulled the girls out, and laid them on the grass. They looked cold and fresh, like wet ivory. When I came back into the house alone, Stephanie took one look at me, sighed, and called the police to report the accident.

•••

A woman from the prison calls and tells me what has happened.

My visit with Lita is being canceled for the day, which disappoints me, but the circumstances excite me. My daughter has been so despondent and withdrawn. I'm thrilled to see her passion for the work has returned. I knew she'd had it in her; I'd never given up.

"She's being separated from the other inmates," the woman says. "At least for a period of time."

"Of course." The sadness in my voice is genuine, but not for the reason she thinks. "When can I see her again?"

There's a sigh on the line that sounds like Velcro tearing away.

"That will be decided at a future date, sir."

"Okay," I say, and before the calls ends I muster the courage to ask one more question, because I have to know. "Will the girl she attacked live?"

The woman's silence tells me my daughter's victim is already dead. When she finally speaks, my mind is too far away to take in most of the words. I am drifting, vacant. Later, when I talk to the attorney, I learn that the other girl was dead before they could even tear Lita off her.

•••

Tracy was the first.

Not just the first born, but also the first to give in to the calling.

She sent a pencil through the eye of a playmate while at daycare. The boy lost the eye, but he lived, which deeply upset my daughter, even though we never scolded her for it. Tracy was too young for any kind of juvenile hall, so she went into the only alternative, which was counseling. This only did her harm, but Stephanie and I were not allowed to pull her out of it. It was part of the agreement of the settlement. We tried to retain the little girl we loved, but she just kept slipping further away from us, the medication and therapy dulling her until she became a husk of her former self. Without a channel for her creativity, without *the work*, all the light had gone from her.

When the day came that she walked off our lawn and into the street, I watched her from the window. My daughter was a faded love letter crumbling in my hands. She looked at me just once, to

7

make sure I was watching, and we both heard the car coming around the corner as she hid behind the tallest bush. She did not turn to say goodbye, but leapt out from behind the bush just in time for the fender to break her in several places, sending her rolling beneath a tire.

•••

The nothingness has already returned to Lita's eyes, glassing them over, and her mouth is curved downward, her skin pasty. She's still allowed out in the yard, but never with fellow inmates. She's alone, always alone. At least for now. And she doesn't get to wear denim anymore. Now she's in an orange jumpsuit so bright it hurts my eyes and makes the flesh on my forehead draw tight. Her arms still have bandages on them. The other girl did her best to defend herself with her fingernails, but she hadn't been able to get out from under Lita, even though my daughter was the smaller of the two.

"I've missed you," I say.

I can tell she's glad to see me even though her face is blank. She's blocked at the moment and is still too young to understand she'll be inspired once again, likely sooner than later. The gaps between grow shorter and shorter each time, but that's something she must learn on her own, just as I did. I put my hand up to the glass, trying to reassure her that nothing is over. She'd felt this way once before, and with her behind bars even I had worried it was true. But my Lita is resourceful, like her mother. And she's so talented, perhaps even more so than Stephanie had been.

When she speaks, her voice is small, a mouse scurrying between ruins.

"Better than Sarah," she says.

I nod.

"That's two now," she tells me.

"Yeah, I know."

I wink at her and color returns to her cheeks. Her shell is a gray and nebulous thing, but she is my child and I can see spring blooming behind the cracked mask of her face. A slight curl in her lips hints at a secret joy, one we share in this moment without the guards knowing. Her tiny smile is a mirror in which I see us on the Ferris wheel again. Lita is three years old and, as she hurls her doll into the night wind, it spins, stark white against the darkness of space and time, and as it tumbles toward the earth the candy lights of the ride color my daughter's face. Her teeth flash like razors and she laughs and screams at her dolly to die.

That's when I'd first known.

The warm memory recedes and I'm back in the stale hollow of the prison.

"Billy never got to try," she says. "It's sad."

"It is."

Billy is the only person I ever loved who died of natural causes, succumbing to sudden infant death syndrome before he was old enough to learn our ways.

"He was the only boy," Lita says. "He could have done so much, taught me so much."

I sigh from deep within my chest. "Well, the past is the past. What matters is what you do *now*. They're all gone, Lita, but we're still here. You've made it, and I'm not going anywhere."

She tilts her head and the light leaves the lenses of her glasses, and now I can see the brilliant blue seas of her eyes. Her pupils are dilated, no longer the pinpoints they were before this latest killing, and her irises writhe around them. In those eyes I can see the powder blue of her mother's eyes, and I remember how Stephanie's pupils had dilated as the last bit of life seeped out of the thirty-nine stab wounds Lita had left in her body. I had come home just in time to hold my wife's hand and see her final smile. She was so happy in that moment, so proud, just as I was and still am.

"We're not done with it all, are we Daddy?" Lita asks.

But it's not really a question. It's a statement, and she's majestic in saying it. My heart combusts with love for her.

She leans on the counter, getting as close to me as she can, and puts her hand on the glass between us. I do the same, our palms pressing flat to each other, and in this moment it does not matter that she's getting older, taller, and budding into a young woman. This is my little girl, my flesh, and we both know she's become my favorite.

MY NAME IS CHAD

IN THE ATTIC WAS A box full of VHS tapes.

Amongst the recorded-off-TV copies of *Rocky III*, *The Worst Witch*, and *The Princess Bride* were a few cassettes labeled: *Home Movies.* Seeing those words written in my late mother's elegant cursive was enough to stroke my heartstrings, so I carried the box down from my parents' attic and into the living room. The house was packed up in preparation to sell it, the stuff I was keeping on one side, donations on the other.

When I pulled out the tapes, I realized a VCR was on the bottom of the box. It had been years since I'd seen one, let alone one of these early models—a large, metal beast heavy enough to hammer railroad spikes with. I remembered it sitting on the shelf below our old tube television with the rabbit ears and the dial that had to be turned with a pair of pliers. Each "home movie" was labeled with years, all mid-1980s, when I'd been just a child. But I couldn't remember having ever watched these tapes. Dad had shot plenty of videos through the years—he'd been obsessed with cameras and gadgets—but the earliest home movies I could remember were from 1989, trips to Disney and Gatlinburg and Universal Studios when it opened the summer of 1990. Dad went digital before most people had, and everything was transferred to computer files and DVDs. I'd already browsed through all of those, nostalgia hitting me like a tsunami in the wake of his death. So it seemed these early VHS tapes had been forgotten about, my folks passing away within a month of each other, leaving this worn out box of memories tucked behind totes of Christmas lights and plastic jack-o-lanterns.

I thought of Janie.

Maybe she was why the tapes were stored and forgotten.

When they'd been alive, Mom and Dad didn't talk about my big sister all that much. Her tragic death at age eight was a tight pocket in their hearts, a smothered memory they never let up for air. Maybe it was too painful to revisit home movies with her in them, but Mom and Dad couldn't bear to throw the tapes away any more than they could bear to watch them.

That my sister might be on these tapes made me eager to view them. My memories of her were so fuzzy and faded. The only clear mental image I had of her was based on the photograph Mom kept on the mantle—a little blond girl with sad eyes, sitting in front of a birthday cake. The harsh contrast had always haunted me. It was as if Janie had somehow known that birthday would be her last. I'd been only seven when my sister was run over by a drunk driver. These tapes offered a rare window, the chance to rewind life itself.

I closed the box and took it home.

•••

Pauline had at least let me take one of the TVs with me when we'd separated. It was one of the few items she didn't fight me on when I moved into an apartment, leaving my wife and two boys in the house I'd been paying off for the last eleven years. It pained me to live apart from Luke and Matt, but I just couldn't forgive my wife for having an affair. Living on my own—for the first time in decades—seemed like the best thing to do, rather than have my sons grow up watching their parents in a toxic relationship. The divorce was still in the works, but I'd been living single for a few months by the time Mom finally passed away, following right behind Dad. I was their only living child, so they'd left me the house. I'd thought about moving into it, but with my divorce looking more and more likely, I needed the money selling it would bring in. It pained me to be parting with the house I'd grown up in, but we all have to move on at some point.

Most of my things were still packed in the apartment, but I'd left the TV out to watch the Mets and the Giants. After hooking up the VCR, I dimmed the lights, setting the mood like I did whenever I watched movies with the boys. I'd even stopped on the way home and bought a bag of popcorn. Whatever was on these tapes was very special. I wanted to give the whole experience the magic it deserved.

I had to adjust the tracking as the first tape began, playing with the buttons until the static and blips smoothed out. I chuckled, wondering what my sons would think of such an archaic device, and damn did it make me feel old. The picture cleared and I sat back in my chair, watching the grainy images whizz by.

Houses and sidewalks moved across the screen. Whoever had been filming this had been shooting from the inside of a moving car. It drove through what appeared to be a residential neighborhood. The treetops were red and gold and dead leaves scurried across the pavement, scratching like cat claws. From the makes and models of the cars on the street, I could tell this footage had indeed been shot in 1986, as the label suggested. Already a warm, blooming sentimentality was rippling through me. The car turned and so did the camera, a school I didn't recognize coming into view. Children trotted down the steps, some hopping along, skipping in excitement. It was an elementary school and apparently the day had just ended.

Mom and Dad must have taped Janie and I coming out of school, I thought. *Maybe it'd been a big day.* The year seemed right for me to have started first grade, and Janie would have been in second or third . . .

. . . and still alive.

The car came to a stop and idled by the curb. A few minutes went by as children exited the school. Buses and station wagons filled up; otherwise nothing was happening.

I slumped in my chair.

"Come on . . ."

I was just about to fast forward when the camera zoomed in and I saw something familiar—a little boy with a dirty blond bowl cut, corduroy pants, and a black and yellow, button-up jacket, the glossy kind that show off sports teams. On the sleeves were patches of superhero logos. I recognized it because I'd had those same patches, that same jacket.

"Holy shit."

That's me.

I watched myself hop down the steps, a metal lunch box in my hand, a backpack high on my shoulders.

Sitting in my chair now, over thirty years after the film was made, I watched Little Me with bittersweet wonder. A sigh left my chest, a tear trickling from the corner of one eye. I expected Little Me to come running toward the camera, hop inside the car, and tell Mom and Dad about his day (it occurred to me then that no one had spoken on the tape yet) but instead he just skipped down the sidewalk to the playground. The camera followed. There was a slender blonde woman in an autumn coat standing by the swing set. Large, '70s-style sunglasses covered her eyes. When Little Me saw her he picked up his pace and she squatted down to greet his open arms. She picked him up and spun him. Little Me laughed with all the light of the world.

I did not recognize the woman at all.

My mother had always been heavyset with dark brown hair. And I'd had no aunts or other relatives who resembled this woman. Even when she took off her sunglasses and put them atop her head, I still couldn't identify her. She could have been a babysitter or family friend I'd long forgotten, but why would Mom and Dad have gone to the school to film someone else picking me up? Before I could ask myself any further questions, the video suddenly cut off, a static pop filling the screen before the next segment began.

It was similar, with Little Me walking down the sidewalk in front of the school and meeting the blonde woman, but their clothes were different, so it had been shot on a different day. This time the car followed them down the street for a while, filming them up until they came to a small house and went inside.

I heard my mother's voice off screen.

"Here we are," she said.

My father's voice followed. "I've got it down."

"Easy access from the rear, it looks like."

"Yeah, the map says so too. Behind is all forest."

There was a silent moment before my mother spoke again.

"Lookin' good."

The video cut off.

I put down my bag of popcorn and sat forward in my chair.

What in the hell is this?

All I could think was that my parents were following around my babysitter, making sure I was okay with her. Parents had been known to set up hidden cameras in their homes to monitor how their children were being taken care of. But we'd lived in the same

13

house all my life, and this place wasn't it. It must have been the woman's house, maybe an in-home daycare center.

There was a blip of video static.

The next clip was filmed in a backyard. There were more leaves on the ground than there'd been in the previous clips. Time had passed. There were bare branches in front of the camera and smaller trees touched by the red and gold of autumn. Whoever was filming was in the woods behind what appeared to be the same house Little Me and the woman had gone into before. The camera was watching Little Me draw with chalk on a blackboard.

Something about this made me shift in my seat. My mouth went dry as I wondered why Dad would be sneaking around in the woods, filming me from afar like a Peeping Tom.

Off camera, Mom spoke.

"This feels right."

Then there was Dad. "Yeah, I think so too, Betty."

Betty?

My mother's name was Ava.

Dad had never called her Betty. No one had.

The warm nostalgia that had filled me was rapidly turning in my stomach, transforming into something black and thick. I felt suddenly and inexplicably anxious, a curious fear creeping from my throat down to my groin.

"I'll hold the camera," Mom said.

Dad grumbled. "Let's just turn it off."

"No, no. This is a *special moment.*"

"Right. So let's not screw it up by—"

"Harry, I want to tape this."

Harry? My father's name was Jackson. *Was this some kind of role-playing?*

Maybe it was a movie. Not a regular home video, but an amateur film. Mom and Dad were acting, playing characters named Betty and Harry. But that didn't make much sense. If that were true, why would they be off camera and mentioning the fact they were using one? So-called "found footage" films weren't a thing back in the 1980s.

"Alright, fine," Dad said. The camera must have been passed to Mom then because the image swirled, showing a gray sky and a blur of rocky terrain. "Just be ready to go when I come back."

"I will, I will."

The camera straightened and pointed at Little Me.

Now I was out of my seat, knees on the floor before the screen. I was sweating.

On the video, a man went charging through the woods. He was so much younger—body thinner, hair thicker—that it took me a moment to recognize my father. He moved swiftly, breaking through the thicket and into the yard where Little Me glanced up, his face white with shock. I swallowed hard seeing the terror in my younger self's eyes. As Dad came upon him, the boy let out a cry and broke into a run.

"What in the hell is this?" I asked the TV.

Dad caught up with Little Me and snatched him into his arms. He didn't pick him up—he *snatched* him, like an armored car robber with a brick of cash. The camera shook slightly and I heard Mom breathing heavy, a few excited whimpers humming out of her.

"Mommy!" Little Me screamed.

Dad came back with the boy kicking him. Little Me was not looking toward the woman holding the camera, but looking back at the house, his arms outstretched as he called out for his mother.

•••

No.

It couldn't be what it looked like. It just couldn't. This had to be a gag or something.

I waited for more, but the tape held only static. I fast-forwarded it to the end before giving up. Nothing. Ejecting the first tape, I went to the second volume labeled 1986 and put it in.

Little Me was somewhere dark. It seemed subterraneous, like a cave or cellar. There was a single light pointed right at his face and he squinted against it. Behind him were only gray and black shadows on damp concrete. I could see only his face and upper body, but it was enough to reveal the straps holding him to the chair he sat in.

I heard my father behind the camera.

"This could be easy, son."

Something about that phrase made the adult me gasp. It sent a jolt of fear from the bowels of my subconscious.

Little Me turned his head, whimpering.

"You're the one making it difficult," Dad told him. "I've got all night."

Something moved across the camera and then slinked back into the shadows. When I heard her voice, I realized it was my mom.

Or whom you thought was your mom.

"Jackson," she said, "don't be so hard on the boy. He'll come around, just like his sister."

I realized she was using the name I'd always known my father by. She held a white board in front of the camera. It read: *Progress report. Chad. November 19th, 1986.*

"I wish he was more like his sister," Dad said. "If he doesn't shape up, he'll have to go."

Go?

I mouthed the word but made no sound, scared, even though what was frightening me had already happened decades ago.

"Don't talk like that," Mom said. "I know he'll work out fine. I won't lose another son."

What? My parents had never mentioned another son. The implications of the tape just kept getting darker.

"Let's just get back to it, Ava."

The board left the screen. Little Me hung his head against the harsh light.

"Alright, kiddo," Dad said, a little patience returning to his voice. "When I call you Chad, you need to respond. It's your name."

Well, yeah, of course, I thought.

This had always been my name. But Little Me mumbled something.

"What was that?" Dad asked.

The boy's voice was so small. "Greg . . . my name is—"

A shadow moved upon Little Me and he screamed. I saw my father's back come into focus as he positioned himself in front of the boy. There was something metal in his hand. He flicked it and a loud crackling sound startled me.

"You know what *that* name gets you!" Dad yelled.

He pushed the metal wand into Little Me's side. The crackling came back, and this time I saw the blue glow of the electrical current just before Dad shocked Little Me with the prod. My younger self twitched in the seat as the electricity ran through him. He was too paralyzed to scream, so I screamed for him. I stood up and turned my back on the screen, unable to bear the harsh reality of what I was seeing. Everything I knew about my family—about myself—was crumbling, revealing the blackest underbelly, a mask being lifted from a face too horrible to look at.

"Say your name!" Dad yelled.

The boy was sobbing, but he managed.

"Chad . . . my name is Chad."

•••

The rest of the tapes documented the whole process.

Little Me was deconstructed and then reprogrammed. My "parents" used torture and rewards to get the boy to not just say what they wanted him to say, but actually *believe it.* They did this expertly. It made me wonder where and how they'd learned to brainwash people like they were the CIA. It was one of many questions I had. My life was a lie—a hologram, a phantom. All there was now was mystery and madness.

My parents were kidnappers.

I was not a son. I was a victim.

I'd been stolen from my mother's yard and tied up in a basement, only being fed when I complied with the alternate reality my captors had created for me. I was zapped with a cattle prod when I resisted. Sometimes I was hit with a belt. Other times ice water was poured over me and I was made to sit like that in the basement, in the dead of winter, until I turned blue. But when I was a good little boy there were toys and games. I was given cookies and allowed to watch *Romper Room* and Saturday morning cartoons. As the tapes went on, I was even allowed out of the basement, and by the second volume of 1987, the progress reports were almost entirely positive. I had my own room, plenty of toys, and seemed to be in a good mood most of the time. The only negative marks (my mother noted them on screen) were for having bad dreams that made me wet the bed. Other than that, I was their precious son, the boy they'd always wanted.

I was healthy. I was happy. I was Chad.

The 1988 video didn't have any progress reports. This was where the home videos began. There were games in the backyard. There were Christmas mornings. There were barbeques, Slip 'N Slides, birthday parties, and little shows I put on for my parents, singing and dancing and telling lame child jokes.

And there was Janie.

There was my older sister with the sad eyes and blonde pigtails. The videos of her were the one thing out of this box of nightmares that brought me any joy, bittersweet though it was, considering all I'd learned. Obviously she wasn't my real sister. That didn't make me love her any less, but it did make me wonder if she'd been Mom and Dad's birth daughter or another hijacked child. That they'd said she'd done better than Little Me during the progress reports indicated the latter. Maybe that's why her eyes were always so sad, even when she was smiling. There was something going on behind them (something I would learn about on the next cassette) but for the moment I was just enjoying seeing her. Tears came when I watched us playing in the yard, but my emotions became twisted and confused when Dad joined us. We all wrestled and laughed, and Little Me looked especially happy, which was exactly how I remembered my childhood. I certainly didn't remember any belt or cattle prods. Memories of my teen years were equally pleasant, just as my adult years with my parents were. I'd always felt I had a warm and loving family, and I'd always been grateful for that.

But the VHS of 1988 volume two started with a return to the basement. This time Little Me wasn't the only one tied up. Janie was right beside him, chained to the radiator. I gasped when I saw the bruises on her arms, the black eye and bloodied lip.

"You sons of bitches," I said, wishing I could travel through time and take my folks by the throat.

It was a horrible feeling to want to harm the people who had raised me, the mother and father I had always loved. But they weren't who I'd thought they were. Dad was a criminal and a sadist. He was a filthy child beater. Mom was no better. This revelation was like losing them all over again. It hurt even worse than normal mourning because it tarnished the sweet memories that make grief bearable.

On the video, Mom spoke first.

"A little liar. All this time, you've been faking, Janie. Don't you know how bad it is for a little girl to lie?"

Janie sniffled but did not cry. Her face was granite. It was a look so alien to a girl that young. She seemed strong beyond her years, even defiant. Though only a child, she wouldn't let these sick people break her down. I wished I could reach through the television and pull her out of that dungeon, out of time itself. She belonged here with me, not imprinted on this painful, forgotten memory.

"We've given you everything," Mom continued, "and how have you chosen to repay us? By lying to us! By acting all this time! Acting like you loved us the way a little girl should love her Mommy and Daddy." She moved into the camera's line of vision, casting a menacing shadow across the children's faces. "You broke our hearts, you little bitch."

Mom smacked her. Little Me cried for her to stop.

"Shut up, Chad! We're not so happy with you either, young man."

"Please, Mommy," he said. "I love you and Pa."

"Yeah, right!" Dad barked off screen. "If you love us so much, why did you go with Janie when she tried to run away?"

Before Little Me could answer, Janie cut in. "It's not his fault. It was my idea. He didn't know where I was taking him."

"And where were you going to take him?" Mom asked. "You think anyone else would have you, huh? You think anyone else would love a couple of ungrateful, sneaky little brats? You should be thankful to have us, but oh, no. Not little miss Janie. She has to be a troublemaker—"

"I just wanna go home!" Janie said. Her face was turning red. She had a breaking point after all. "I want my Mommy and Daddy!"

So she'd been kidnapped too. Only her mind didn't fold as easily as Little Me's had. She'd played along with their illusion of a family, gaining just enough trust and freedom to be able to make her escape when the time was right. And, God bless her, she'd tried to rescue me too.

Mom zapped her with the prod.

"Brat," she said, shaking her head. "Nothing but a brat."

Mom turned to the camera. Her face, while younger and smoother, was more horrible to me than I could have ever dreamed possible. In the darkness of her eyes I saw only bottomless cruelty and selfishness. She was a demon, a monster.

"We're never going to get her where she needs to be," she said to Dad. "You know that, don't you?"

Now it was Dad who showed sympathy. "Come on, Ava."

Their change of names made sense to me now. Aliases, just in case . . .

"I know she's Daddy's little girl," Mom said, "but she's trouble. Chad is such a good boy now. He's not a faker like her. We don't need her being a bad influence, or worse yet, taking him away from us. The next time she sneaks him out at night, we might not be lucky enough to catch them. I mean, we were just about to put them in public school."

I heard Dad sigh. "You're right, hon."

19

And that was the end of Janie.

•••

There'd been no drunk driver. Hell, there hadn't even been a car accident. I know because I saw the video. It was through a flood of tears, but I saw what happened to my big sister on September 14th, 1988. It was the last of the tapes I could bring myself to watch that night. Days later, I would see that all the other home videos were just as normal and joyous as I remember my life always being. There were no more progress reports or punishments, only my happy little family for thirty years' worth of footage.

Stopping the VCR, I clicked off the TV and went into the bathroom. I sat on the toilet and sobbed, using up half a roll of bath tissue. I hadn't cried that hard in a long time, not when I'd caught Paulina in her infidelity, not even when I'd buried my parents. This was a heavier, deeper grief, and beyond the sadness there was only horror.

When I finally gained control of myself, I put on my shoes and grabbed my keys. I always put on music while driving, but tonight I didn't on my way back to my parents' house, so all I heard was the sound of the shovel I'd put in the truck's bed, clanking back and forth as I went around every turn, going faster than I should have.

Pulling into the driveway, the house was dark in more ways than one now. I felt none of the warm nostalgia it had always filled me with, especially once I'd left home for college. My every return visit had made me feel so safe, so loved. Now I felt like I was stepping into the pit of a ghoul. This was not a family house, but a haunted house, a place where horror had nestled in and made its home. On the porch, my hand shook as I tried to get the key into the deadbolt. I felt dizzy and nauseated and had to remind myself to breathe as I leaned on the shovel for support.

"Please . . ."

I so wanted to be wrong. Despite everything I'd seen on those tapes, I still wanted it to be some elaborate scary movie my parents had been making. I wanted it all to be a lie, a vicious prank someone was playing on me with CGI and masterful editing. Denial was the last lingering thread of my sanity.

I just wanted my family back.

Nothing happened when I flicked the light switch. I'd forgotten I'd canceled the electric. This made me think of the cattle prod and I winced, pushing the memory out of my mind. There was no moon tonight and thick ropes of blackness hollowed the hallway. There was a faint, stale odor here—old people, old carpet, old pain. Though it was a warm night, a chill crept across my vertebrae and I held the shovel out with both hands like a weapon, as if I could fight off the house's evil history. But my only real weapons against it were my love for my sister and a determination to uncover the truth, no matter how much it hurt to expose it.

At the door to the basement I went to the ledge where the flashlight was kept. There'd been one on that ledge for as long as I could remember. Even when the bright overhead light had been on, there were corners down here that were always swallowed by shadow. I flicked on the flashlight, descended the short staircase, and entered the childhood torture chamber my mind had blacked out to protect me. There was a richer smell down here—wet earth, black mold, sorrow. When the flashlight's beam landed on the radiator, I quickly turned it away so not to have to see where Janie had died. Before I could lose my nerve, I placed the flashlight on the floor to illuminate the spot I'd seen on the video, and sent the tip of the shovel between a crack in the tile.

I dug.

•••

Two small skeletons.

Two children, dead for decades, buried beneath my parents' house.

I stood above the shallow grave, looking down at Janie and the brother or sister I never knew. Bones and dirt and two little skulls.

I turned away and retched. It brought me to my knees. Anguish was like a blade turning in my guts, a wound on my very soul. I wanted to burn the place down, to set ablaze this hell house, as if that could erase what had happened inside of it.

But of course I couldn't do that.

Selling this place meant money to get me through my divorce. It meant a substantial increase in my children's college funds. I couldn't burn it down, and I couldn't report what I'd found to the police. Nor did I wish to. The house would drastically depreciate in value if it became known as a "murder house," and I sure as shit didn't want to be known as the hijacked foster son of a child-killing duo. I'd wanted to find the truth, but now that I had, I knew it was to be a very private truth, one I would take to my own grave one day.

Janie's real family may have appreciated closure, sure. But after thirty years, perhaps it was best to leave things buried where they were, figuratively as well as literally. At least that's what I tried to tell myself. The same went for the family of the mystery child in the hole, and the same went for my birth mother, my *real* mother. Did I have a real *father*? He hadn't been on the videos, but he must have existed, even if he and my mother were separated. How long had they looked for me before succumbing to the brutal truth, and how devastating had the ruination been? Had their marriage crumbled? Had they become alcoholics? One of them might have spiraled into drugs and overdosed. One may have committed suicide, unable to deal with the staggering loss. At best, after three long decades, they were elderly if not dead. And after all that time, they must have moved on in one way or another, learning to cope with the grief, for better or worse.

We all have to move on at some point.

Or maybe they were still looking. Maybe they never gave up hope.

There were many reasons why they and the authorities may not have been successful in finding me. For all I knew, I'd been kidnapped from a whole other state, maybe even country. As far as I could remember, I'd always lived in upstate New York, but my memories had proved unreliable. What if the thin, blonde woman from the videos—the one who had scooped up Little Me in her arms every day after school—was still searching for her lost child? What if the hope that I was still out there was all that kept her going? Didn't my real mother deserve the same truth I'd been so desperate to unearth? She could be half mad from the pain of not knowing what had happened to her son, not knowing if he were dead or alive.

My flesh shivered as I realized there might have been a funeral for me. It seemed likely. But that made sense now, didn't it? I was alive, but the boy who'd been swiped from that backyard didn't really exist anymore.

Part of me wanted to find this woman who had given birth to me, who had been robbed of the chance to raise me and watch me grow up. But another, bigger part of me was afraid of how painful that would be, how alien it would all feel. No matter the blood ties, we were strangers. All that bound us now was tragedy. Besides, searching for her would mean going to the police with what I'd discovered. That was a whole other form of digging things up, one

I couldn't endure for a variety of reasons. Being with his mother is what Little Me would have wanted. But I wasn't that child anymore.

There was no Greg.

My name is Chad.

I looked down into the hole. The fragments of children who'd lost even more than I had looked like bits of chalk in the dim light, like the kind Janie and I used to draw on the sidewalks with on those long summer afternoons. One skull was turned to the side, its lower jaw detached. The other was intact, facing up, and I was able to see the hole in the top of the skull where they had shot my sister.

"Goodbye, my family."

I started refilling the grave.

WOMB

SOLOMON LOOKED UP FROM HIS stitching to watch his sister as she slid the butcher knife in and out of the young woman's mouth. The blade glistened like red morning dew as it danced in the mangled hole of human meat. The lips were shredded to pulp, the gums bleeding, many of the teeth having been knocked out with the hammer. The girl's mouth was in fleshy tatters and bits of cheek were falling from her face as the knife sawed away.

"Fuck you, bitch!" his sister shouted.

The victim could only moan behind a gargle of blood.

"You ain't pretty no more!"

He liked seeing Seri get excited like this. His sister's bloodlust always led to sexual lust, and that suited Solomon just fine. He was happy to provide her murder victims if it got her in the mood to let him climb on top of her again, or vice versa, if he was really lucky. But while he appreciated the horniness the killings gave his sister, Solomon took no joy in the murders. They were simply mandatory, an unfortunate necessity to his work, his need, his yearning. And of the two of them, he was the only one capable of initiating them. He was fat but stocky, a 300-pound juggernaut with brute strength and the muscle they needed to dominate victims. Seri could only partake in the maiming and torturing she so enjoyed because Solomon would nab the women first and drag them back to the attic. She was too weak to do this on her own.

While they were twins, they had opposite body types, her being so thin that she appeared skeletal, particularly because of her pale skin and baby-fine hair. Not only was she too frail to get a victim back to the house, but she was a total shut-in. Solomon hated going outside, but he was able to do it. His sister, however, would suffer a complete mental breakdown by even going into their spacious and secluded backyard. Sometimes it had been like pulling teeth trying to get her to even leave her room.

Seri laughed as she ripped another tooth from the crying girl chained to the dresser. It was typical of Seri to destroy the faces of the young women he collected, especially when they were pretty like this one. Born with a harelip and a birthmark that purpled half of her face, Seri was terribly self-conscious about her looks and seethed with envy at women she deemed prettier than herself, which was every one of them.

Solomon had often tried to no avail to assure her she was beautiful, and he meant it too. She was the only woman for him, the only one who would ever arouse or understand him.

The only one other than mother, that is.

"It's a shame you can't see how ugly you are now," Seri said to her victim.

She'd already gouged out the poor girl's eyes with a filed-down spoon.

His sister turned to him, smiling a corpse rictus. In the dim light that came through the attic's large, oval window, her nightgown looked black with the blood. When they locked eyes, she lifted the skirt of the gown up over her boney legs, then higher, showing him her overgrown bush. Coils of sweaty blonde winked at him like fish eyes.

"There's work to be done," he said, showing her what he had been stitching.

"Come on, baby. Who's my big boy?"

She began to play with herself, her bloody hand turning her pubes pink. She lifted the gown higher still, teasing him with her jutting hips, wishbones that always granted his wish.

"It's time for naughties," she said. "Time to make a no-no!"

She turned around and bent over, her pimply, pancake bottom so chalky white it appeared to glow in the murk. He stood up, fumbling with the tape of his diaper, the weight of his belly familiar on his forearm.

With the prisoner bleeding beneath them, Solomon entered his sister like he had so many times before, and with each thrust he made, she made an equal thrust with the knife, pushing it deeper down the girl's throat.

•••

With the little bitch dead and their lovemaking over, Seri powdered her brother's bottom and closed the fresh diaper. He was getting bigger. Soon they might have to switch to some sort of homemade cloth diaper unless they could find XXXL disposables for adults.

But Solomon needed to be the baby. That was his thing. The diapers, the bibs, and the bonnet were not just what got him off, it was what made him feel secure, just like the walls of the house made her feel.

Whenever Seri was made to leave the house, she felt like a child who woke up alone in their bed during a thunderstorm, pulling the blankets up high, only to have someone under the bed make a grab for them. Panic would seize her and make her retreat into her mind in a horrible daydream. She would lock up and leave her body as the world outside of her head became distorted and freakish.

Or maybe that's just how the world really is, she thought.

So she babied Solomon—even though he was ten minutes older than she was—and went along with his plan for the attic. She didn't share his passion for what they were doing with the dead bodies, but she sure enjoyed making them. Killing brought her to new heights of ecstasy and the torture of their young victims gave her a feeling of pitch-black euphoria. In an odd way it made her feel closer to her mother too, and that helped to soothe the wound of her passing. It helped her to deal with it a little easier. And that was why she understood Solomon's need to do what he was doing. He missed mother too, and he had his own way of coping.

"We have to get back to the stitching," he said.

He stood up, seeming antsy.

"Alright," Seri said. "Where do you want me to start?"

He looked to the piles of gore floating in the open foam coolers. On his workbench, a flayed uterus lay waiting. Draped over the chair was the quilt of breasts he'd been working on before their afternoon delight.

"I'll get back to this," he said. "But first let's get the girl to the tub. You need to drain her."

The mansion was equipped with several bathrooms, but their mother's had the largest standing tub. It was perfect for tossing the bodies in, where they could work the limbs like pumps to drain them of blood. That was Seri's job. She also did the initial slicing and dicing. She could take the flesh from the bones and expunge the guts, but when it came to separating limbs she needed her brother's help.

Solomon undid the chains on the body and lifted it by the arm-pits. Post-mortal feces exited the dead girl in a wet plop and her feet slid through it as he dragged her toward the stairwell. Just a few weeks ago, the smell would have repulsed Seri, despite how often she changed Solomon. But now, given the state of the attic, she'd become immune to odors.

•••

The staple-gun worked best when it came to lining the walls.

Flesh likes to tear, so it was always difficult to get it to stay up there, but he'd learned by trial and error the staples were the best way to go.

This latest victim gave him enough flesh and innards to complete the east wall of the attic. He stood back, admiring his work. The entire wall was covered in suspended flesh and female reproductive organs. Breasts were also included in the mélange, but not for sexual reasons. That was why he didn't have any lips or anuses. This wasn't about sex; this was about the insides of a woman, with a touch of their nurturing mammary glands. Most of the flesh was turned inside out—showing the pulpy, red under-side—making the attic into a meat cocoon. Fallopian tubes dangled like gelatinous ribbons and ovaries swam in the pink like watermelon seeds.

This wall was still fresh—still wet even—and it felt so soft on his fingertips, so pure. Comfort enclosed him. He felt cradled, a puppy in the arms of an adoring little girl. The wall behind him was also complete, but the meat was turning now and attracting flies, which was inevitable. He tried not to be too much of a sour-puss about it. After all, the important thing was that it was almost done. All that remained was the small rear wall, and the one at the front, which would be easy to cover because the window took up most of the space.

That was what he'd saved all the vaginal lips and pubic hairs for.

The opening.

The birth canal that let light into the womb.

•••

"How many more do you think?" Seri asked.

She was picking at her food again, unable to handle the idea of putting any of it in her mouth. It was spaghetti with butter, her favorite, and still the thought of eating made her want to gag.

"More what?" her brother asked.

"Don't tease."

He grinned over his third helping and slurped a noodle into his mouth, buttery spittle spraying from his lips like a dolphin's blowhole. He drank more of his warm milk before answering.

"One, two at the most."

Seri's heart sank. "And then what?"

He gave her a puzzled look.

"Then we can go home," he said.

"We are home, silly-billy."

"I mean our true home. The home we shared before this world."

"The *womb?*"

"Yes."

She wanted to tell him it wasn't really a womb he was building and that they could never go back to being fetuses, but it was too strong a dream of his for her to shatter. Not only would he never accept it, but she also felt it would be cruel to try to deprive him of what he valued most.

But she had needs too.

"What are we going to do in there?" she asked.

"Everything. *Anything.* We'll be home again, sissy. We'll finally be safe; safe from all of the things mother protected us from when she was alive."

"She kept us in the house . . ."

"But that wasn't safe enough, was it? It wasn't as warm and assuring. I'd give anything to be back inside of mother. But it's too late now, isn't it?"

Seri had long thought her brother and mother had maintained a secret sexual affair. But the idea of Solomon being with anyone else—even their beloved mother—made her feel sick and hollow inside, so she never pried for the truth. It was better to live in denial and let the suspicions turn to rage she could always release upon the pretty, young girls.

"The womb we've made," he said, "that's the closest we'll ever

28

come to being with her again. I wish her body had been enough to fill the whole attic, but it wasn't, now was it? The attic is small but it needs more bodies to get it right. Wrapping myself in mother's flesh made me feel a little better, but it's just not the same as the security of a womb you can really live in. I know you don't remember the joy of being in the womb, but I do, and it's something I've spent my whole life pining for."

Seri moved her plate away and crossed her hands on the table.

"What about me, big brother?"

"You'll be right there with me. We'll be back in paradise and . . ."

"I mean what about what I want? You'll be getting what you want. What about me?"

For once, Solomon stopped eating. "The womb is not enough for you?"

His slate eyes were bloodshot and deep, the bottom of a cold, merciless sea.

"The womb will be great," she assured him, even though it wasn't how she really felt. "But what about the girls?"

"We'll be finished with all of that business."

"But . . . but why?"

"We'll have no need for them anymore."

"I still will!"

"What for?"

"Because I like it when you bring them home. I like giving them *makeovers*."

"You don't understand, sissy. Once we're in the room we won't have such needs and desires. We'll be whole, entirely. It will be so peaceful—to want for nothing."

"Nothing? No needs at all?"

"It will be pure contentment."

"So what? No more girls? I don't get to have my fun? Hell, what about making nasties with you? You gonna take your pee-pee away from me too?"

Her brother looked genuinely stunned, an ape seeing itself in a mirror for the first time.

"You don't understand," he said.

"No, you don't!" She stood up and the chair scudded loudly across the hardwood. "I want things, Sol. I need things. I can't go without playing doctor with you. And now that I've been killing all these girls, I don't think I can go back to not doing it. It makes *me* feel the way the womb must make *you* feel. It makes me feel that much closer to mother."

There was a silence between them then.

"Why is that?" he asked.

"Come on, Sol."

"No. Tell me."

"You know how she was. How she *really* was."

Solomon looked way. It was typical of him to do this, to act like mother never had this side to her. She was his holy grail, perfect and pure. She couldn't possibly have been soiled by the same dark desires she had instilled in her offspring. Not in his eyes. It infuriated Seri sometimes, like it did now.

"You knew about them just like I did," she said. "All those kittens and puppies she adopted. All the field mice she took from the meadow. You found pieces of them all around the house too."

Solomon stood up. He was silent for another moment and then started to walk away from the table.

"Don't do this to me," Seri said.

He kept on walking, back to the stairwell, back to his womb.

"Sol! The day you stop bringing me girls is the day I stop changing your diapers, you hear me? You'll have to clean up your own boom-booms!"

The attic door slammed.

•••

"I'm sorry," he said.

He was sodomizing her, slowly and lovingly. Just the way she liked it.

Solomon always knew how to make an apology. And she knew he could never give up making no-nos.

"I'm gonna get another one tonight," he said. "You can have all the fun you want with her, I won't even rush you. I know I've rushed you a time or two before. Well, not this time. This time it's all about you."

"Deeper," she said, and he complied.

She sunk her fingernails into the headboard of their mother's bed.

"What about when the womb is done?" she asked.

"Just give it a chance. That's all I ask. If you don't feel totally at peace, then we can work something out."

"More girls?"

"If that's what it takes to make you happy. But I don't think

30

you'll need them. You'll see. The womb will be our Garden of Eden. We'll be one again."

Thinking about it gave him such pleasure she felt his cock go completely solid. As her anus stretched, she felt her colon flush with semen.

"That's my good boy," she said.

She poured some of the talc into her hand and reached between her legs to powder his balls.

•••

The woman kicked violently. Her movements were crazed as he carried her up the stairs, and he was relieved he'd at least gotten the handcuffs on her before the drug had started to wear off. Normally he would have seriously crippled them by now, but he wanted this bitch to be as intact and cognizant as possible, so his sister could get as much pleasure out of her as she wanted.

He felt he owed her that much.

She'd been so helpful with the womb. She understood it, understood him.

Soon she would also understand they had no more need for these sluts and schoolgirls, these weak and unchallenging prey. The bliss of pre-birth awaited them in the bloody, closed-in space above. Seri just didn't have the vision to foresee it as he did. Once it was completed, he was confident the awe would send shockwaves through her, filling her with the holy light religion promised but never delivered.

"Let me go, you fat motherfucker!"

The girl's kick connected with his knee and he felt it begin to buckle. He braced himself against the wall but she started to slip from his grasp so he leaned forward in the other direction, slamming them into the opposite wall. He wrapped his fingers in her long hair and used it for a handle as he bashed her skull into the drywall a few times. He was careful to use the side of her head so not to spoil the face for Seri.

He was such a good brother.

Having heard the commotion, Seri opened the door and reached down to help him hoist the girl into the attic. She'd abandoned her kicking in favor of sobbing. Seri took her by the hair just as he had and used it to slide her across the floor. When the girl's eyes opened and saw what surrounded them, her skin went white as a silent scream twisted her face. Solomon knew it was just this sort of look that got his sister wet.

Seri cackled and dropped to her knees, lifting the hammer over the girl's head with the opposite end facing down.

•••

Together they took the intestines out of her, doing a tug of war with the body, making the guts unfurl like a hose from a spool. The gash in her belly burped and fizzed. Once they were removed, Solomon stepped forward with the shears he'd filed to be as sharp as straight razors.

Flies were everywhere, planting their own eggs in the dank womb. The sound of their buzzing created a sort of sick ambience. Seri found their drone to be serene in its way, but she had always liked insects. In her bedroom she still had the collection she'd obtained as a child. There were the labeled critters on the special board, a collection bought for her as a birthday gift, and then there were her shoeboxes she had filled with the butterflies and spiders she'd managed to catch and imprison. She'd let them all die slowly, and kept them all, her own eight-legged treasures and colorful transformers.

But these flies weren't pinned in place and curled onto their backs in a cardboard container. They were a frenetic army. Seri wondered how her brother felt about their presence. It seemed to her the attic was becoming less of a womb and more of a hive.

Solomon seemed not to notice.

He cut into the body with gusto, showing the same enthusiasm he'd had when they first dug mother out of her grave.

Watching as the meat piled up beside him, she realized it would be enough to finish covering the remaining walls. Solomon had even taken care of the ceiling, leaving only the floor, which was covered in bones and entrails anyway.

By morning, he'd have his womb, and then he would be happy—finally, *finally* happy.

•••

It wasn't enough.

It was beautiful, like fine art made from finer flesh, but it wasn't enough. Something wasn't quite right.

Solomon huffed and sulked, watching the morning light knife through the blinds on the oval opening of the womb, the vaginal lips that covered them looking like swollen slugs.

Where's the bliss? Where is the euphoria? I'm back in the womb. I'm not just a baby now; I am pre-born. This was the dream, so why doesn't it feel like a dream?

He sat there naked and ran his fingers across the fleshy wall. He pressed his cheek against it, feeling it stick to his face.

He could almost cry.

"What's wrong?" Seri asked.

He'd forgotten she was even there.

"I don't know."

"This is what you wanted, isn't it?"

"You know it is. But something's off. It's incomplete somehow."

"Maybe we need another girl."

Christ, is that all she ever thinks about?

"You're not giving this a serious chance!"

Seri scoffed. "Hey, it's not even doing it for you, why should it do anything for me?"

"Maybe if you kept an open mind it would be working right now. Maybe it's your doubt that's holding it back!"

"Don't put this on me! I did everything you asked me to!"

"Well, *something's* not right."

Seri looked around. "The wall you started with is really rotting now. Some of the innards have turned black and are covered in maggots. Maybe we need fresh meat to replace it."

"Are you insane? That rotting meat is *our mother*, remember?"

Seri looked away in shame, a child caught in a lie.

"Besides," he said, "by the time we get new flesh on that wall the other ones will be rotting. It's an endless circle and you know it. You just want me to keep delivering little whores to satisfy your bloodlust."

"Hey! That's not fair. I want you to be happy too, Sol. I want you to have your precious womb, I just don't know what more you want from me!"

Seri stormed off, thundering her way down the stairs, leaving him alone in his womb—his stinking, rotting womb.

Maybe she was right. Their mother's flesh was merely sludge now, and it was the most important flesh of all because it was flesh of his flesh, blood of his blood. The right flesh was not just meat he could lift from the streets.

Flesh was sacred.

Flesh was *family.*

An epiphany washed over him like a river of blood.

•••

"I love you," her brother said as he hit her again.

Tears rolled down his giant head.

"Don't do this, Sol!" Seri cried.

But the chain was already out.

"You were right," he told her. "The flesh needs to be fresh. But I need it to be genuine, as close to mother's flesh as possible to recreate her womb."

"Don't kill me . . ."

"You're as close as I can get, sissy. Your insides, your pussy, your uterus—all as close a match to mother's as any will ever be. I need you, Seri. I need you now more than ever."

She tried to twist away from him but he was far too strong. Panic had always pummeled her when she would leave the house, but now it was panic that made her want to do so for the first time.

"We can try something else!" she cried. "We'll get it right together, but not like this!"

The chain slid around her waist.

"It's the only way to complete the womb," he said.

Begging him wouldn't work. She had to take a different approach.

"Who's gonna take care of you? Who's gonna powder and burp my little baby? Who's gonna kiss his boo-boos and play with his pee-pee?"

This slowed him down for just a moment, but he shook it off.

"We'll be one, sissy. You'll see. I'll be re-born through you, just as if you pushed me out from between your own legs."

She thrashed now, kicking and screaming like all the bimbos he'd brought home for slaughter. But she wasn't one of those human cattle. She was his sister and his lover, the only one he had left. How could he think killing her would solve his problems? It could only make them worse, for now he would be alone with the memories that haunted him, alone in this dusty old mansion— alone with his madness.

When he leaned over her to snap on the handcuffs, she saw her chance and took it.

His nipple came off between her teeth.

•••

Solomon couldn't understand why she was fighting it.

Why would she want to stay in this misery when utopia awaited them both? Here she had a chance to not just be in the womb but to be *of* the womb, to be the most important part of it. Her sinew and lovely genitals would be his silken doorway into a new birth. It wasn't just about staying in the womb. He realized that now. It was about the womb giving him a second chance at truly being an infant once again—clean and free of all the lust and envy and fear and despair. He would be pure in all the ways he'd failed to be the first time around, and that was the womb's ultimate power and purpose. By making this possible through her sacrifice, Seri would be the ultimate mother. She would give birth to her own brother, thereby surpassing their mother. It was not just the passing of a torch from a matriarch to her daughter; it was the taking of a throne. Once and for all, the children would have come together to be worthy of their mother's love.

But Seri didn't understand that.

She just wasn't the visionary he was.

But it would come to her in time.

She spat his nipple into the air, a mad grimace making her sunken face seem all the more skeletal, eyes whirling in their black pits.

"You must deliver me," he said.

Before he could snap the lock on the chains a knee went into his groin and his balls sent hot daggers into his every nerve ending. As he recoiled, Seri came up with the chain and swung for his face. He just barely ducked under it.

For such a small and frail woman, she was an absolute energy bomb, and before he could straighten up she had wrapped the chain around his neck and was pulling it tight like a noose. He struggled to get his fingers beneath the loops.

"You don't wanna get me no more girls to kill?" she asked. "You just wanna kill me instead? Maybe I'll get my rocks off by killing you then!"

He tried to twist away but she jumped onto his back and wrapped her legs around his waist, tucking them under his undulating gut so she could get them all the way around. The chain tightened as she sunk her teeth into his ear. When he tried to roar all that came out was wheezing. He writhed, a horse trying to buck its rider, but Seri held tight, using the chain like reins. He tried to throw his arms behind him to punch her, but his back was so wide and his arms so fat he couldn't reach that far. His own blubber slowed and blocked him, so even when his fist connected with her there wasn't enough power behind the blow to knock her off.

Solomon ran backward to slam her against the wall, using his weight to push the wind out of her. The spongy flesh of the womb wall cushioned the blow, but still he could hear her brittle bones cracking inside of her chest. She began to gasp in short, pained breaths and he wondered if a snapped rib had punctured one of her lungs.

Still, the chain tightened. He could barely breathe now.

She bit into his other ear and began chewing.

Solomon grabbed his sister's ankles and pulled her legs up high. He did this with great and sudden force, planting his elbows on her knees so they'd stay locked in place as he snapped her legs to each side. They broke like dead tree branches. She screamed in his ear and the chain loosened as her legs dangled, swinging and flopping, assuring him they'd separated from the joints.

He reached beneath the chain and began to slide it off, but Seri stayed on his back, reached for his face and dug her fingernails in. Her middle fingers gouged into his eyes, the nails twisting, forcing one of them out so it dangled upon his cheek like a misplaced testicle. He reached for her hands and she dragged her fingernails across his face, shredding and mauling, and reached into his mouth and began pulling his bottom lip down, the nails working like dull fishing hooks.

He was blinded by blood as he reached behind his head and managed to grab a handful of hair. Their mutual battle cries filled the womb, making a horrible cacophony with the thrum of the flies that filled the attic in a tenebrous fog. Solomon charged forward, a prodded bull out for blood, and he tumbled forward with his sister's head in his hands, trying to flip her forward and off him. But she reached into his mouth and grabbed both sides of his cheeks as she sunk her teeth into the sweaty fold of his neck, clinging to him like a hungry tick.

Charging forward blindly, Solomon crashed through the oval window with Seri on his back, brother and sister forced through the fleshy opening of the womb, a length of bloody chain binding them like an umbilical cord. Spilling out of the darkness and into the broad daylight of the real world, they tumbled from the peak of the towering mansion, spilling and falling, reborn.

KIN

AT LEAST HIS WIFE WAS no longer with him, so she wouldn't have to see this. She would try and make excuses for Bobby, just like always. Well, nothing could excuse the boy now. Merle no longer cared if he was their only son; Bobby had to die. It wouldn't be easy for him, but a father has responsibilities, and a man's gotta do what . . .

He tried to concentrate on loading the 12-gauge. Years ago, he'd bought it for hunting. He and his black Labrador, Buster, were two of the best fowl hunters in all of Dale County, even if Merle's buddies hated to admit it. Merle had never dreamed he'd be using those same skills to track a man, let alone his own boy.

But Bobby wasn't a boy anymore. He was twenty-two, even if he'd never stopped acting like some damned teenager. He'd been in and out of jail so many times Merle had lost count. He'd also stopped bailing Bobby out of a cell some time ago, but that hadn't deterred his son from continuing to sell dope and moonshine, steal anything that wasn't on a chain, and generally get drunk and cause trouble.

But now . . . what he'd done now . . .

Bobby had gone down to the bog, and when he came back, he did so silently. Merle never heard his Jeep pull up. Strangely, he'd walked home. The boy's sister had been right outside. Merle hadn't heard a single scream.

No stint in jail would be strong enough punishment, and there was no death penalty in West Virginia. No police this time. This was a family affair, and Merle was going to take care of it using the old ways, the honor code that had been passed down from generation to generation and still held fast here in the backwoods beyond the Appalachian Mountains.

Abigail entered the kitchen. She'd been the one to find Merle's daughter, Sunny. Abigail was Merle's thirteen-year-old niece, and she'd always looked up to her older cousin and had received all of her hand-me-downs over the years. The girl shouldn't have had to see Sunny like that. Merle was grateful that his brother had kept him out of the barn, where what was left of Sunny's body lay.

"Daddy's gone on home to git some flashlights 'n such," Abigail said. Tucked into the belt of her jeans was the .22 she'd gotten for her twelfth birthday. "Says he'll meet us in the basin."

"What bout ya Mama?"

"She'll be along. Daddy done called her to leave work early." Rita was a cashier down at the grocery mart off rural route 9. "She's gonna stop at the house and git the dogs."

Merle slung the belt of shells over his shoulder. The calcium deposits in his knuckles sent a familiar ache through his fingers. He slung on his fishing vest and put his old army hat on his grayed head.

Abigail stepped closer, as if she were going to approach him, but then leaned against the wall with her head bowed.

"Uncle Merle?" Her eyes were wet and they couldn't hold his gaze. "I'm just . . . I'm just so . . ."

He put his hand on her shoulder. "I know."

She gave him a weak smile, looking so much like Sunny that it tore something deep within his chest.

He was ready to kill his son.

•••

An hour and a half earlier, Abigail had gone into the barn to return the axe she'd borrowed to chop logs for the coming winter. It was lighter than the one her father owned, so she was better able to handle it.

It was a good thing she'd had it too.

Opening the door, Abigail stepped into the gray light of the barn, and the first thing she noticed was the terrible odor. It was like a horrible amalgamation of septic tank, rotting sweet potatoes, and old ground beef. She gagged and covered her mouth and nostrils with the front of her flannel shirt.

That's when she heard the ripping sounds. She wondered then, from the sounds and the acrid smell, if her cousins were skinning a deer. Moving toward the back of the barn where they did all of the dressing, her eyes adjusted to the shadows. She followed the noise, but didn't call anyone's name, a sudden intuition giving her reservations. Not knowing why she was scared, she moved gingerly, the axe held close to her chest. As a little girl she'd hated the dark, especially when it came to barns and sheds. She'd felt she'd long gotten over it, but now it had crept back up like a spider in her belly. She gulped dryly, the ripping growing louder as she rounded the corner. When she first saw the body, and Bobby disemboweling it, she thought it was a deer. But she quickly realized her error when she saw Sunny's face . . . or what was left of it.

She hung by her ankles from the chainfall that ran from the rafter above. Her torso was slit open from her gullet to her sex, and Bobby was expunging her insides with a blade from an old mower. The rest of her body was covered in cuts and abrasions, spotted by mud and wet leaves. The steel tub was beneath her, half-filled with fresh gore.

A nauseated cry came out of Abigail.

Bobby turned to her, his face spattered with his sister's blood. His eyes were wild and glaring beneath a tight brow, seeming somehow radiant. It looked like he'd been rolling in grass. He was green and dirty. Twigs stuck in his skin. He stood, saying nothing, the mower blade in his hand dragging a length of viscera. Abigail had not been raised to take chances and didn't bother to warn Bobby. She swung the axe immediately, and in dodging it Bobby slipped in blood and fell over, landing in the tub with a splash.

Abigail ran, not looking back all the way home.

Once there, she could barely tell Daddy what had happened. She was shaking and out of breath, nearly delirious with shock. Abigail doubted he would even believe her, for she didn't even believe it herself. When she started to let it out, Daddy slapped her. He'd thought she was fibbing, just as she'd assumed he would. But she persisted, and when she saw the anger in his face turn to dread she knew they'd be going to the closet armory before they headed back to Uncle Merle's house across the field.

When they got there, Bobby was gone, leaving only a bloody trail that led toward the low valley where scraggily paths wound through the glade until the woods grew denser, giving way to the bog. Daddy went into the barn alone and Abigail heard him vomit. When he came back out, his face was as white as the keys on Meemaw's piano. His bushy moustache accentuated his frown.

"Should I git Uncle Merle?" she asked.

He shook his head. "Nah, let me handle this."

•••

Merle, Abigail, and Buster waited in the basin for Merle's brother, Darrel, and when they heard his Ranger crackling down the path they walked toward the clearing of the open country, their boots sucked by the mud that had formed after last night's rain. The sky above them was slate, the color of a hone for skinning tools. Bobby's jeep was parked along the edge of the woods, doors wide open, rifle still in the back. Darrel came out of his truck with his own Remington, the earflaps of his hat sticking out at the sides, flannel shirt buttoned wrong so it hung lopsided. Merle wondered if he was drunk again.

"Sure ya want her comin?" Merle asked.

"Reckon she's old nuff."

Barks echoed from the other side of the hill, along with the dragon's growl of a V8 engine. Rita's pickup rumbled down the slope, the bloodhounds in back with their faces flapping in the wind. They knew a trip to the valley meant hunting, and they were exploding with anticipation. Seeing his friends, Buster's paws danced. Rita had her radio turned up, Hank Jr. singing his new hit about his country state of mind, and the truck's overhead lights cut the grayness like poltergeists from an old movie. She pulled up beside her husband's truck and the dogs jumped through the hole where the tailgate had once been, greeting everyone with sniffs and licks.

Rita's eyes were like wounds. "I can't believe it. I'm so sorry, Merle."

He nodded to his sister-in-law. She was a fine woman. He sometimes wondered what she saw in his deadbeat brother. She had leathery skin from too much hard work in the sun, and her sleeves were rolled up, tattoos having aged to obscurity, both hands holding a double-barrel shotgun.

"Well," he said, pointing to the marsh, "let's git in there. Don't want that sumbitch gittin any farther away."

•••

The throat of the woods seemed to open for them, the wet foliage curling like broken fingers. The same chill that had overcome Abigail when she'd entered the barn returned to her, clenching her lungs so her breathing quickened.

Her uncle looked at her with more concern than Daddy ever would.

"Ya alright, child?"

"Yesum."

She carried her pistol in one hand. Compared to the adults' weapons, hers felt suddenly small and inadequate. In her other hand she held Otto's leash, the bloodhound pulling against the prong collar, nose deep in the muddy trail.

Daddy used his rifle to point at some footprints. "Dems his cowboy boots."

The prints did look like boots to Abigail, but the spacing of them was off. They seemed too far apart, spread so wide Bobby must have been walking and doing splits at the same time. Going forward they were gaped, as if he'd been leaping.

"Don't that look weird?" she said.

Daddy ignored her. "This here's all mud. Hope them boys can sniff him without much crushed grass."

The dogs huffed in reply and Abigail followed her family as they weaved off the trail and into the gray thicket. It was still early afternoon, but the insects were singing now, their song sounding different somehow, electric and warped like radio static. Abigail's skin prickled and she caught up to Mama, who looked at her and tried to smile despite the gravity of what they were doing.

"It's gonna be alright, sugar."

Abigail nodded. Mama knew best.

•••

It was all wrong.

They were wandering on and off the trail, the footprints never running in a straight line. It was like the boy was playing hopscotch with himself. Merle gritted his teeth at the idea of Bobby skipping through the brush like a frog after what he'd done. His hands ached for his son's neck. He'd brought a rope for it too.

The sky sulked behind the sorrow of the trees. The gray had gone grayer. So had he.

Buster was off the leash, but unlike the bloodhounds, he was staying at Merle's side. This was odd behavior for the dog. Normally he would be bounding through the woods in search of their prey. Today his tail hung flat and he kept looking behind them.

"What?" he asked the dog.

Buster looked at him with eyes sad enough to reflect what was in Merle's heart.

"Think he done headed for the bog," Darrel said.

Rita's face was pinched. "Wash himself of sin."

Merle shook his head. "Ain't no washin this away."

He glanced at Abigail. He could see the fear in his niece's pale face and wished he could talk his brother into sending her back. But Darrel wanted to grow her up and show her just how mean the world could be. He thought if she got familiar with the danger that stalked young girls around every corner, she would be better able to avoid it. Merle wondered if in these woods she'd get a little too familiar with it.

There was a rustle up ahead and some low branches swung. The dogs started barking and everyone raised their weapons, even Abigail. The trees were spaced out. They should have been able to see what had bolted past, but Merle caught nothing, not even a blur or shadow. He turned on his flashlight. Rita did the same with hers. They scanned the russet bramble but nothing surfaced.

"Possum, maybe," said Darrel.

Rita shook her head. "Them branches are mighty high for a possum."

"Woman, ya got sumpin better?"

Merle shushed them, listening. In the distance he heard a sound like yogurt being stirred, only louder.

"What the Sam Hell is that?" Abigail whispered.

Buster started whining.

"Come on," Darrel said.

They followed him, the mud growing thicker. Merle wished he'd put on his clodhoppers instead of his riding boots. He'd been in too much of a hurry, too frazzled. His nerves were still cutting him like razors so he put a Marlboro to his lips. Before he could light it, Abigail touched his arm.

"Don't," she said.

"Why not?"

"The cherry. He'll see us."

He almost told her they weren't in the trenches in Nam, fighting the yellow man like he had twenty-five years ago. Lord, was 1961 really a quarter century behind him? Bobby didn't even have a gun that they knew of. And with the noise of the dogs, he would know their position anyway. But sensing Abigail's nervousness, he tucked the cig back into his pack.

"Let them boys go," Darrel said.

Rita removed Max's leash and he dove between the trees in the direction of the slurping sounds. Buster didn't follow Max as he normally would have. His hackles were raised and he seemed to sense something the senior dog didn't. However, Otis was ready. He was honking at the end of his leash, but Abigail was reluctant to release him.

Darrel turned to her. "Little girl, I said let em go! Now set Otis free fore I box ya ears!"

Rita's eyes fell on her daughter with silent apology. Abigail's chest caved, and she unlatched the leash, Otis springing forward like he was jumping into a swimming pool. Mud kicked up and spattered Merle's legs as the dog followed its brother. Dusk was a ways off, and yet the world around them seemed blacker now, dense and thrumming with the screams of crickets. Merle could see his breath. It had grown cold so fast.

"Whadda bout Buster?" Darrel asked. "Aintcha gonna sic em?"

"Don't think he's feelin right today."

But then again, who was?

•••

Abigail didn't like this. She could no longer see or even hear her dogs. Max was a good ol boy, but Otis would always be her baby, even if he weighed eighty-five pounds now. She'd raised him up from a pup and he still slept in her bed every night no matter how stinky he'd gotten during the day. Whenever he was running he was louder than a monster truck rally. She should be able to hear him. But there was no noise coming from the thicket ahead, only the strange, sucking sound that reminded her of searching for the last bit of a milkshake with a straw. Either whatever was causing the noise was getting closer, or they were getting closer to it.

"Spread out," Daddy whispered.

She went with him while Mama went with Uncle Merle. Mama gave her the flashlight.

"Daddy, where's Otis and Max?"

"Don't worry now, darlin. They's huntin."

He was trying to reassure her, but she could see the worry in his bleary eyes. Daddy wasn't much for love, but he kissed those dogs more than he ever did her or even Mama. Abigail buttoned her coat. The cold was getting meaner and she wished she'd brought gloves and earmuffs. At least she had a scarf on. When she looked over her shoulder, she could no longer see the others. Mama, Uncle Merle, and Buster had vanished behind a grove of pines. She didn't like being separated from them. It made her feel even more vulnerable. The image of her flayed cousin kept popping back to the front of her mind no matter how hard she tried to shove it out. She'd been scared before—of the bear that had wandered into a campsite, of the snake that had surprised her while she was cutting grass, and even of her Daddy when he'd had one too many Jack and Cokes. But these were dangers she could understand. What Bobby had done was something she could not make sense of, something she never would have dreamed him capable of. That's what frightened her the most—how alien he had seemed. If she didn't know better, she could almost swear it wasn't even him, that some maniac had put on Bobby's skin before killing Sunny.

Daddy stopped suddenly and Abigail's breath caught in her throat.

"What is—"

Daddy shushed her.

She realized the wet, churning sound had stopped. Something was jangling now, sounding like pocket change. Her body tensed as she saw a black mass shifting behind the bushes, and she put both hands on her .22. Daddy raised the rifle to his shoulder, the small flashlight on the base of it zeroing in on the brush.

"Come on outta there!"

Branches crackled as Max pushed through, his collar chiming. Daddy lowered his Remington and sighed with relief.

He walked toward the dog. "Where ya been, ol boy?"

Max snapped at him and bared his teeth, his eyes glowing a swampy green in the light. Abigail shivered. Daddy stood up straight, confused and insulted by the dog's aggression.

"Max?"

Abigail smelled something sharp on the air, the same wet penny smell from the barn.

"Daddy . . ." She reached for him but was too afraid of Max to move forward. The dog seemed no more like himself than Bobby had earlier that day. "Daddy, don't."

But Daddy never was one to listen to her. He was proud of how he'd trained his dogs and wouldn't tolerate disobedience. Max snarled as he approached. Abigail saw blood on the dog's teeth and snout.

Daddy scowled. "Max! It's me, ya damn mutt!"

Their trusted pet lunged.

•••

Buster turned his head in the direction the rest of the family had gone. He whimpered and Merle stopped for a moment to listen but heard nothing but the steady thrum of the insects and that horrible slurping.

"Sumpin's wrong here," he said to his sister-in-law.

Rita looked at him, swaying.

"Ya alright, Rita?"

She blinked as if she had just woken up, seeming disoriented. Rita mumbled. "What's . . . what're we doin?"

"Ya don't remember?"

When she looked at him, her eyes seemed to reflect a light that had no source. He raised the flashlight and flinched, seeing the lime-colored fungus speckled on her neck. Bits of algae stuck to her black hair as if she'd just emerged from pond scum.

"Judas Priest," he said, "what'n hell done got on ya?"

He reached for her and she grabbed him by the wrist with surprising strength.

"Ya've always wanted to put yer hands on me, aintcha, Merly-boy?"

He tried to pull away, but she clenched tighter, her fingernails poking into his wrist.

"What're ya talkin bout?"

"I seen the way ya lookit me!"

"Come on, now, I ain't been lookin at ya no way cept the right way."

She shoved him away. He ran his flashlight up and down her. Rita's clothes were clean but her exposed skin was various shades of green, patches of it fuzzy like an old sweater.

"How'd that gunk git on ya?" he asked.

And *when*?

Rita looked at her blotchy arms. Her brow furrowed.

"What gunk?"

That's when Merle heard the first gunshot of the afternoon.

•••

Abigail screamed as the bullet hit Max. Her hands were shaking but she'd still managed to connect with her target. It deeply pained her to shoot the dog, but she had to stop it from mauling Daddy's arm. When Daddy had fallen, he'd dropped his rifle while trying to pull Max off him. Abigail had to get close to shoot the dog without risking shooting Daddy by mistake. The round from the .22 rattled Max but he did not whimper or relent. He kept on growling, so Abigail shot him in the head. He died instantly and his body crumpled into the mud.

"Tarnation!" Daddy said.

The sleeve of his flannel was ripped away and his arm had deep punctures where Max had sunk his teeth in and shook his head as if he'd had a duck in his jaws. Abigail wished they'd thought to bring a first aid kit. She knelt down beside her father, took the scarf from around her neck and wrapped it around his wound. He flinched at her touch.

"I can't believe it," he said. "Ain't like he ain't got his rabies shot."

Max had never been aggressive to anyone, let alone his owner.

"He's got blood on him," Abigail said.

"Course he does," Daddy said, hoisting his arm.

"Naw, I mean he done had blood on him fore he bit ya."

Now that Max was lying on his side, they could see the green spots covering his body like a rash. Abigail's heart hammered against her ribs. That ominous intuition was rising in her again, trapping fear in her gullet. She helped her father up and he stared down at his dead best friend, his posture sagging.

She looked all around them. "Daddy, where's Otis?"

•••

Merle barely had time to push the barrel of her shotgun away. The blast made his left ear go dead, but he'd managed to avoid the spray. Buster was barking his head off. When Merle looked into Rita's eyes, he saw that the lashes had become splintered twigs. Her face was mossy like tree bark, snarling teeth blackened by a sticky substance. When her mouth moved it sounded like the yogurt noise they'd been hearing.

"What's wrong with ya?" he yelled as they wrestled.

Rita was stronger than he would have expected. While never a weak woman, he didn't anticipate she could challenge him physically. She pushed him backward and he barely maintained his balance. They spun together and collided with a tree. This took the wind out of Rita, and Merle managed to pry the shotgun from her hands.

"Have ya gone mad?"

She didn't reply. She looked behind Merle at his own shotgun, which he had dropped on the ground to fight off her attack. Merle raised the barrels at her chest.

"Don't even think bout it."

"How ya gonna tell yer brother ya done kilt his wife? Whatcha gonna say to Abby?"

Merle's scalp drew tight. Rita reached to her side slowly, and when she undid the holster of her buck knife, he cocked the hammers back.

"Dang it, Rita. I ain't kiddin. Don't makes me drop ya."

She slid the knife out, sneering.

"Why ya doin this?" he asked.

But Rita wasn't giving him an answer any more than she was giving him a choice.

•••

Tears poured down Abigail's cheeks. They'd found him behind a line of bushes. Something had ripped Otis apart. It looked as if a pack of bears had attacked him. Daddy cursed a blue streak and was only silenced by the shotgun blast that echoed through the marsh.

"Oh God," Abigail cried.

She muttered a prayer and Daddy took her by the arm.

"Stay close to me now," he whispered.

This part of the woods was dark, but now she saw that what she'd thought were shadows on his face were actually some sort of green scabs.

"Daddy?"

He shushed her and they moved faster, even as the mud fought against their feet, trying harder and harder to swallow them into the earth. Dense mist rose from the ground like dry ice, swirling in pale jade whips around their ankles, and she could feel its arctic touch even through her boots. Its color perplexed her. It reminded her of swamp gas, but they weren't close enough to the bog for that, were they?

There was a crackle in the bushes and she aimed the flashlight just in time to see something large and spindly move between the trees. She shrieked and Daddy fired. The shots filled the growing darkness with quick bursts of light in which they saw the creature climbing the branches. It looked like some sort of plant life, but it moved like a man—a fast, nimble one. The creature bleated a wet scream, and Abigail knew what the sucking sound had been.

Daddy fired again and bark splintered away but the monster

kept climbing higher, dodging the light of Abigail's flashlight just when she'd catch it. When they lost sight of it entirely, a great shadow swooped over them, and they looked up to see the thing spring like a monkey from one tree to the next. While twisted at odd angles, the limbs and torso seemed human, but the body was sprouting branches and leaves. She hit it with the beam of her flashlight, and despite his fish eyes and mouthful of tar, she recognized her cousin.

•••

"We'll git ya to a hospital," Merle said.

Rita lay with her back against the tree, struggling to breathe as she wrapped her arms around the wound in her stomach. Blood had soaked all the way through her coat.

"Why, Rita?" he asked, choking on tears. "Why'd ya have to try'n stab me?"

She made clicking noises. "K-k-i . . ."

Buster barked at her, the hair on his spine a mohawk.

"I'm gonna git help," he told her. "I'll drive on back to the house 'n call 911."

He didn't want to move her, fearing it would release her viscera. He'd seen enough gut shots in Nam to know she didn't stand much of a chance, but he had to try. Despite what she'd done, she was family, and somehow he knew the green fuzz all over her was responsible for her having turned against him. She was sick with something he could not identify, something that had messed with her brain.

She was trying to speak. Dark goo dribbled down her chin.

"K-k-i . . ."

Merle grabbed both guns. He wanted to leave one for her to keep the animals away, but couldn't trust her not to shoot him in the back when he walked off.

"I promise I'll be back for ya."

Rita opened her arms, pulling her entrails out like red wings.

"Kin!" she screamed. "*K-k-kiiiiinnnn!*"

Merle ran.

•••

"I swear it was Bobby!" Abigail cried.

"Nah. That was some kinda . . . swamp beast."

"I done seen his face! Sumpin's happened to him. He ain't Bobby no more."

"Nah." Daddy shook his head. "Can't be."

"But Daddy, whadda bout Max? He changed too. He was all mossy. If he'd a-had nuff time, he mighta turned into a swamp monster too."

When her father turned to face her, she saw a new sheen of slime dripping from his hairline like emerald sweat. She tensed and took a step back.

Daddy sneered. "Yer talkin foolish, girl."

"Please, Daddy. Bobby killed his sister, and Max killed his brother. Sumpin out here's changin everybody."

She never saw his backhand coming. She staggered at the impact, tasting blood as her lips hit her teeth.

"Shut your trap, missy," Daddy said. "Don'tchu *ever* talk that kinda trash bout the family!"

He moved upon her, eyes gleaming. She'd seen violence on his face before, but this was different. His expression throttled her with terror. She kept the flashlight on him, trying to blind him, her other hand sweating around the handle of her .22. She held it low, still unwilling to point it at someone unless she planned to fire. This was still her Daddy.

She decided to run.

A moment later something whizzed by her ear. He was so close the sound of the air splitting came before the crack of her father's rifle.

•••

Merle's breaths burst out of him, cold sweat rolling down his brow.

He hadn't run so fast or so long since he was in his thirties. His knees sent pins of fire into his marrow and a tight ball of pain twisted in his side; but he kept running, the horror of what he'd seen fueling his blood. Buster kept checking back with him as he led them to the trail.

"Take me to the others, boy."

He wanted to call out for the rest of his family, but was too frightened to do so. An air of evil had closed around the swampland. He could sense it in the unseasonable cold and early darkness, see it in the low fog drifting at his ankles. He couldn't explain what was happening, but he knew the family had to get out of there. He was grateful for Buster, especially now that his flashlight was dying. Above him, the trees rustled even though there was no wind. Merle looked up. A black mass swung. He froze and switched off the dim flashlight so he would be harder to find, but

Buster was growling, giving away their position. The darkness swooped down upon them like a massive bat and they moved just in time to avoid being crushed beneath whatever it was. It rose up on its haunches, and in the dim light Merle saw legs stretched far apart and arms crooked like pipe cleaners. The crippled thing had camouflaged itself with leaves.

Merle raised his shotgun. He'd already tossed Rita's in the brush so he could pump new rounds into his own.

"Don't move," he said.

When the creature spoke, its voice was familiar, but one he had not heard in decades. It was high and innocent, and it took Merle a moment to realize it was Bobby's, the voice he'd had when he was still a child.

"Pa," the creature said, "don't fight it."

Between words, the thing slurped and gargled.

Merle's eyes misted. "Judas Priest . . . boy, what's happened to ya?"

The Bobby-creature's eyes were like a mackerel's.

"The bog," it said, "it's lettin me in—to the other side. It's black there, Pa. So peaceful—like sleep, but forever."

Merle's skin prickled. "Son, that's death."

"Lemme take ya with me."

"Like ya took Sunny?" Merle said, hands tightening around his weapon.

"Spring follows winter. Death brings new life."

"She was your own sister! Your own—"

"*Kin*," the creature hissed.

All around them the marsh wavered. Buster barked at the moving trees.

"I takes the same blood that runs in my veins," the creature said.

Merle shook his head. "Whatever all's in these woods has done tricked ya, boy. It's turnin us on our own kind."

The creature's fingers coiled like roots, twisting into the air.

"Its gotta feed," it said, "and I gotta feed it."

His jaw unhinged and black foam sizzled between his teeth.

Something charged through the brush and Merle turned his weapon but recognized his niece's terror-stricken face just in time.

"Help!" she screamed.

The creature's tendrils came at him, slithering around his arms and torso, branching off to wrap around his legs. Merle fired. The creature's body burst in a spray of bark and leaves, but the coils only tightened. Merle's arms were caught. He couldn't pump another round into the chamber. The bushes opened and he spotted Darrel, but did not like what he saw.

Buster left the ground and bit into the Bobby-creature's throat. His jaws pierced the wood coating, and the creature shrieked as bloody sap poured from his gullet. The coils loosened around Merle and went after the dog, so Merle pumped and fired low, taking out the creature's leg. It crumpled and Buster was able to break free.

Merle looked at his brother again, noting the moss that completely hid his features. The man was aiming his rifle at his daughter she scrambled in a pit of mud. Merle ignored the creature's branches at his ankles, shooting at his brother instead, sending Darrel flying backward in a green splatter. Merle kicked away the tendrils and ran to his niece.

"Have ya been hit?"

Tears ran down her cheeks. "Don't reckon."

He tried to help her up and sank into the vacuum of the mud. The ground wasn't just slowing them down; it was trying to pull them down *into* it. Buster barked from the edge of the pit. Merle saw the Bobby-creature struggling, leaves and vines stifling its movements as brackish muck oozed from its orifices. Merle couldn't tell if it was dying or being reborn. He didn't want to wait around to find out. Having no choice but to drop his weapon, he grabbed Abigail's arm with one hand and reached out to Buster with the other. The dog came close and Merle clutched his collar. Buster's muscles flexed as he walked backward, pulling Merle from the mud trying to swallow him.

"Atta boy."

Once Merle got an elbow on harder earth, he pulled Abigail and she clung to his arm. They got to their feet and stepped away from the sinkhole. It was growing. Merle saw his shotgun disappear. Trees and bushes fell, the earth caving, and Buster ran ahead, barking back at them. Merle knew the dog could sense sturdier ground. He was trying to guide them out.

"Come on," Merle said.

Abigail moved forward and he kept himself between her and the creature. It was slithering in an effort to rise out of the muck, but its injury had made it so it could no longer stand, and everything its tendrils grabbed kept bending toward the sinkhole.

Merle glanced at his brother's rifle, but the dark quicksand was tugging at his heels now. There was no time. They followed Buster up the slope just as the woods devoured what remained of Merle's son.

They rounded a corner and a bullet hit the tree they'd stepped behind. Merle turned to see his brother had risen, even though there was a hole in his belly Merle could see straight through.

"Oh, God!" Abigail cried.

They ran. Buster was making a path for them through rockier terrain. It was more difficult to maneuver, but it was harder ground and Merle trusted it would not turn to quicksand as easily. A bullet cut through his clothes and made him bleed; he wasn't sure if it had gone in or merely grazed him. He had to put both hands on his knee to push himself over a boulder and saw that the hair on the backs of his hands had turned to green mold. When he moaned, phlegm filled his throat.

It was happening.

Abigail and Buster were on the other side of the boulder, waiting in the valley basin, both calling to him. Through the layers of fog, he saw the silhouettes of the trucks.

"Uncle Merle, hurry!"

"Go on!" he yelled. "There's a spare key in a magnet box under the bumper of my truck."

The girl cried. "I can't leave ya!"

"Ya better do it!"

"I can't. You're my kin!"

He sighed. "That's why ya gotta run!" He raised his hands to show her how green they'd become and saw the fear in her eyes. "Ya don't run, and I'm gonna hurt ya."

Buster growled at him for the first time ever.

Abigail shook her head. "What?"

"Whatever this is, it wants us to kill our kin! Bobby let it in, and now everyone in his bloodline is gettin infected right along with him. Ya gotta run, Abby!"

Merle registered the hurt in Abigail's face just before something struck his head, and then he saw nothing, and never would again.

•••

Buster whimpered when Merle fell, but he nipped at Abigail's boot, telling her to hurry. The sight of Uncle Merle's head opening had frozen her. Daddy rose over the boulder. Only it wasn't

Daddy. Her father's belly had been hollowed out, but he was empowered by whatever had risen from the swamp to destroy them. He was looking at Uncle Merle and hadn't spotted her yet.

Abigail's hands were shaking so badly she could barely aim. She didn't pull the trigger, but squeezed it instead, using Daddy's shooting lessons in order to murder him. His body jerked as she emptied the .22, tufts of dirt rising from his wounds in place of blood. As he fell, she and Buster ran down the slope, and then she rolled the rest of the way down, losing the pistol, which was out of bullets anyhow. When at last she stopped, Buster licked at her face to get her moving again and she got to her feet and peered through the mist, spotting the trucks. She took a step forward and a pair of floodlights pierced the dusk. Abigail heard the V8 rumble and the squeal of tires as the truck charged at her.

She and Buster just barely had time to throw themselves out of the way. She got up quickly. Mama's truck was circling back. The closest shelter was Bobby's jeep, so she sprinted toward it with Buster right beside her. If the door hadn't already been open, they wouldn't have had enough time to jump in before the truck slammed into the jeep, spinning it completely around, raining glass and other shrapnel all about them. Abigail was rattled but unharmed save for a few scratches, and Buster was still up and barking. The truck was trying to back up but the front bumper was caught in the twisted metal of the jeep. She saw Mama's face behind the cracked windshield, green and menacing. Abigail didn't have time to mourn her. Instead she turned to escape through the other door, and saw Bobby's rifle resting on the backseat. Her cry was strangled as she reached for it, and the truck came free, dragging the jeep's fender with it. She raised the rifle to her shoulder, praying it was loaded.

As her mother switched gears, Abigail fired again and again, the truck's windshield bursting into spider webs. A balloon of blood appeared in the cracks. The horn wailed. Beside her, Buster panted.

"Come on, boy."

They climbed out, Abigail taking the rifle with her. They kept their distance from Mama's truck, but she looked its way as they walked, and saw her mother's dead body hanging partly out the driver's side window. Her hair was sea moss, her face nothing but bloody grass.

Abigail studied her own hands.

They were white, clear.

She pulled up the bottom of her coat and exposed her belly, seeing nothing but normal skin, and when she petted Buster, he showed no hesitation to be with her. She lifted the magnetic box from the bumper and took out the key. Climbing into his truck, she thought about her uncle's final words, and for the first time in her life she was glad she'd been adopted.

NANA'S SECRET

SHE FOUND IT IN THE basement.

Laura was going through all of her grandmother's possessions, all of which now belonged to her. With her mother in the asylum and no other relatives, she'd been her Nana's sole heir, inheriting the colonial house and everything in it. There was antique furniture in the living room, a built-in bookshelf in the den, a standing tub in the master bath and a massive canopy bed in the bedroom. The roof had a small window that looked out into the sprawling, gray woods and beneath the house was the large basement, the walls of which were lined with boxes and totes, except for the east wall, which served as a wine cellar.

Laura was down there, smiling at the warm sentimentality as she sifted through old photos, vintage clothing, and porcelain dolls. The pain of her loss was still fresh even though they'd already buried Nana, but being close to all of these relics comforted Laura, cushioning her from her grieving. They reminded her of just how special Nana had been. Laura had never known her father and her mother was a basket case, so Nana was more of a parent to Laura than anyone else. She had grown up in this house and its sentimental value was far greater than its ample weight in dollars. Over the years the area's property value had skyrocketed, the house easily worth more than $200,000, but Laura could never dream of selling it.

Once it had been signed over to her, she'd been tempted to call her partner, Mia, at the base, but decided she'd rather wait for her to come home from her deployment next month and surprise her with their new home. Mia knew about her Nana's passing, and she'd regretted she couldn't leave the base to attend the services, but Laura had kept her lips sealed about the inheritance, despite how difficult it had been. Mia would never even think to ask about anything monetary. She just expressed her condolences to Laura tenderly, which reminded Laura why she'd fallen in love with her.

When Laura came to the particularly heavy box, she opened it up and at first was unable to identify what was inside. All she saw was glistening wood. With some difficulty she wiggled it loose from the cardboard and set it down. Undoing the bubble wrap, she saw the slick oak and the cheesecloth in the slats, and knew then what she was looking at.

Nana's old tube radio.

It was a cathedral style model from the mid-'40s, with dark brown knobs and a glass dial that lit up with the image of a globe. It was in immaculate condition for its age, but that didn't surprise her. Nana had always taken excellent care of her things. She kept a spotless house and all of her collectible china and statues were kept behind protective glass. Laura remembered the radio being a centerpiece in the living room while growing up, until a CD player had finally replaced it. She hadn't seen it since she was a child and the sight, smell, and feel of it in her hands brought nostalgic tears. She sniffled, picked it up, and placed it on the workbench. Plugging it in, she switched it on, smiling at the booze-hued glow. Through a layer of static she could even make out voices.

It still works!

She turned it off for the time being, wondering if it could be converted to play MP3s. After all, Mia was an engineer in the army. Laura ran her hand along its smooth base and felt a sense of calm come over her. It was a feeling of being home, one she'd never felt in all those crummy apartments, including the one she currently shared with Mia. Nana's house held a special magic which, although it came with sadness now that she was gone, was still unmatchable. There was an energy that came off it, even in the dank of the basement, letting Laura know, deep in her heart, Nana was still with her.

•••

With the help of her friend Sami and her boyfriend, Charlie, she managed to get all of the big stuff out of the apartment and into the garage, where it would stay for the time being. She wanted to wait for Mia so they could decide what to keep and what to give to the Salvation Army. All that was left now was to pack up the little things.

Charlie's eyes were wide and roaming. "Man, this place is incredible."

They were sitting on Nana's leather sofa, sharing a superb 2008 Almaviva Puente Alto, which she'd used to coax them into helping her move.

"This *wine* is incredible," Sami said.

Laura was happy she'd impressed her with one of Nana's gems. Sami was a serious wine snob, having worked at a vineyard when she'd lived in Lake Elsinore, and while she currently worked at a bar that brewed its own craft beers, wine remained her true passion.

"It's the least I could do."

This was truer than they knew. This bottle was worth around ninety dollars—no small amount of change. But there were bottles down below Nana had held on to for decades, some of which could easy sell for four digits. And that was only the wine. She could slap a five-digit price tag on some of the antiques in the house and nobody would argue. On top of all of this, Nana had left her a small fortune in bonds and a lump sum from her life insurance policy. She'd not been this wealthy when Laura was a child, but over the years she'd amassed moderate riches. Laura was overwhelmed by the notion of now being a fairly wealthy woman herself. Mia brought in more money than she did. Laura was almost thirty but still working at the department store she'd started at after college. She was assistant manager now, but the pay was still low and the retail hours were long and unpredictable. Realizing she could now afford to quit and take time to find something more rewarding made her feel like she was ten years younger.

So let Sami guzzle the wine. There was more where that came from.

This basement was full of surprises.

•••

Rain pelted the windows.

The afternoon storms came regularly in the spring months and would go on until night came. Then the thunder would roll in with its lion roars drumming the house. The chandeliers would flicker and Laura found herself fetching some of Nana's gas lanterns a time or two. She had one of them with her now, just in case the lights went out. Dusk had fallen and with the rain coming down there would be no moon or stars, only the black pall of night.

She managed to sort about half of what was in the basement, uncovering some true treasures and a lot of junk clearly entombed for a reason. She didn't see herself needing stacks of old cooking magazines, so that began the garbage pile. She was in the basement for hours, the musky smell starting to make her lightheaded and congested. She wondered if there was mold down there and figured she should get it inspected. She also made a mental note to buy an air purifier. Deciding she was due for a break, she grabbed a nice white wine and headed for the stairs.

That's when the tube radio clicked on.

First its globe lit up, basking her in its shine. Then she saw the arrow-hand in the dial start to spin slowly, a weathercock in a summer breeze. The crackle of static grew louder. She was about to turn it off when she heard the voices again. They were clearer this time, even through the distortion.

"She is . . ." a woman said, ". . . and ready."

The words were occasionally drowned out by moments of fuzz, making for broken sentences. Another woman's voice came on, saying something unintelligible. It sounded like "chain bag."

The third voice was familiar.

At first she'd thought the radio had been picking up a local signal, perhaps from the college radio station or possibly NPR. But now she was far more curious about what she was hearing.

Nana's voice shuddered the cheesecloth.

"Make . . . preparations . . . only the beginning . . ."

•••

It sounded exactly like Laura's grandmother, crazy as that seemed. Only it wasn't the old, trembling voice she'd had in her final years. This was the voice she'd had as a younger woman; the voice Laura had grown up hearing. There could be no mistaking it, or so she thought. There was no recording hooked up to the tube radio. She checked when she'd heard the voice, unplugging it from the wall and taking the back piece off with a screwdriver in order to look inside. So someone out there must have a similar voice to her late Nana—*extremely* similar. It sent a chill down her spine when she heard it, and with the tube put back together, she again plugged it in but only heard static even as she turned every dial on the base. Many times a power surge in a thunderstorm had caused electronics to turn off, but she had never seen it turn one on.

But now that she'd heard her Nana she knew she'd have to listen for more. She wasn't superstitious or even religious. She didn't believe in ghosts. But the idea that Nana could somehow communicate with her made her fill with sweet tears. She knew the very idea was ludicrous, but her grandmother had died very suddenly and Laura hadn't had a chance to say goodbye. Any opportunity to do so would have comforted her in her grief. So, silly or not, she'd be back to try to dial in her voice, or at least try and figure out whose voice had imitated Nana's so well.

But she wasn't going to do it in the dark.

Not with the electricity acting up.

•••

Having so much work to do in the basement, she left the radio down there. The next morning she turned it on while she worked but only heard soft buzzing like an electric shaver. She couldn't pick up any voices or music, the dial just spinning through kilocycles of dead air. Another storm had crept in, and its whistling wind made the branches of a bush rap at the window like a woodpecker. Before the first drop fell, a heavy thunder groaned like the breath of a Greek god, making the ceiling shudder and small bits of dust sprinkle her hair.

On cue, the radio came alive with voices.

Turning to it, Laura watched as the yellow glow of the dial changed to lime green and then to a metallic blue that reminded her of the sapphire earrings her grandmother had always worn. To Laura's surprise it was Nana she heard first, and this time she knew without any doubt it was her voice. The transmission was clearer, with only a faint whizzing of distortion, but the words were still broken up.

"... bestow their ..." Nana said.

"... the chalice ... the book ..." said another woman.

There was a clinking sound followed by the ringing of a small bell.

Nana said something that sounded like "Ask Roth."

"... renounce ... son ..." a man's voice said. He sounded like he was crying.

There was the humming of a small choir.

"No!" the man cried.

The signal went dead.

•••

"It sounded like some sort of prayer," she told Sami over the phone. "It was like they were doing a baptism or something like that. But Nana was never religious, not that I remember."

"Well, who knows what it really was."

"Sure sounded like her."

"She's on your mind a lot. It's only natural that things remind you of her."

"It's more than that. It sounded *exactly* like her."

"And you're sure it's not a recording?"

"Nothing's hooked up to it."

"Well, maybe your grandmother did a radio show or a podcast or something and someone's playing it."

"Nah. She never did anything like that."

"You'd be surprised. I thought I knew everything about my father, but when he died and we went through all of his things we found out a lot of stuff he'd never mentioned. It's incredible the things that people just keep to themselves, Laura. I guess we all have our demons."

•••

The woolsack rattled.

Laura undid the rope and the bag opened, revealing something black and shimmering within. Behind her the radio was offering only a crackling drone but she kept it on, eager for more. She reached into the sack and felt slick material. Pulling out the first article, she saw it was a leather vest. Studs and spikes lined the shoulders and red lace coiled up the front.

What is this, a Halloween costume?

She reached in for the next item and found a captain's hat— also black leather. It looked like the ones Nazis wore in the movies.

Okay, this has *to be a costume.*

The next item was also leather, but far more interesting.

She dropped the bullwhip to the floor.

What the hell?

Digging deeper, Laura discovered what the rattling had been. First, she thought it was just a set of heavy chains but when she got them all the way out she realized there were rusty shackles attached to the ends. Below these were several clamps and vices.

This must have belonged to someone else.

Flipping the empty bag over, she found a tag sticking out of the seam.

Property of Lavern Arthur, it read, as if mocking her with Nana's name.

She backed away, glancing at the other three sacks.

That's enough weirdness for one night, Laura.

•••

"So your grandmother had a kinky side. Big deal."

They were sitting on the porch, sipping the Italian chardonnay. Laura sighed. Sami was getting a kick out of this.

"Now look, there is no way my Nana was a dominatrix or something. That is just *too* unlike her."

"Come on, Laura. If she'd been into whips and chains she certainly wouldn't have told her *granddaughter* about it. Maybe it was just a phase anyway. Maybe she hung up her whip in the 70s."

"She was no *sex fiend.* I don't remember her even dating men after my grandfather disappeared."

Sami turned to her, her mouth slack with shock. "Disappeared?"

"Yeah. When I was a little girl."

"You never told me that."

Laura looked away. "It's not exactly the kind of thing you talk about, now is it?"

"Guess not. But what happened?"

"Nobody knows, really. He was never found, but we had a funeral for him after eight months had gone by."

"I'm sorry. I didn't know."

"It's okay. I honestly don't remember him all that much, just his kind face and his big, goofy glasses."

"Gosh, it must've been so hard for your grandma."

"That's what I mean. She didn't date after that. She was old fashioned, you know?"

"Sure."

In the distance the clouds grew thicker like the bloats of some hellish fire. Though it had not come yet, already the air smelled of rain and was heavy with the energy of the oncoming gale.

Sami nodded at the clouds. "I'd better get going. Don't want to get caught up in what's coming."

•••

A lightning flash brought the radio to life.

61

Laura wasn't even sorting through things now. The radio was her only focus and she kept her phone with her so she could record whatever she heard next. She'd brought the radio upstairs for a while but couldn't even pick up the sound of fuzz. The dial went dark. Once back downstairs it rose to a shining yellow and the static intensified, vibrating the planks.

A woman's sultry moan came on. "Lord of light."

The words came out clear and unbroken. The dial regained its blue hue, casting the basement in the strange incandescence, creating an ultraviolet phantasmagoria.

"Face the altar," Nana said. "Join the circle of snakes."

Snakes?

The echo of an organ rose up like a lost soul. Nana went on.

"God of this world, god of this flesh, god of my mind."

This really is some kind of church thing.

"I am yours," Nana said. "I am myself, whether I am true to myself or not."

"Hail," a group said.

Hail? Not amen *but* hail*?*

"Rise up. Fill my soul with thy power. Strengthen me, that I may persevere in my service and act as an agent of thy works, a vessel of thy will."

There was the sound of chimes. A bell rang thrice. Nana's voice came back, loud and ferocious.

"Bartzabel! Elelogap! Mersilde, guide us!"

The radio crackled and Laura watched in astonishment as slivers of electricity rose from out of the dial and snaked around the planks, making the cheesecloth blow about. The thin bolts of lightning danced upon the tube radio as if it was a plasma ball.

"Hail!" the others chanted.

A woman let out a bloodcurdling scream.

"We offer this virgin sacrifice!" Nana yelled. "We offer her flesh in your great name!"

"Hail Astaroth!" the crowd roared, before the radio fell silent.

•••

She sat in the enormous bed, playing the recording again and again even as she grew queasy hearing it all. This time Laura had a pen ready so she could jot down the names.

Bartzabel. Elelogap. Mersilde.

She went online and typed in *Bartzabel.*

An encyclopedia of demonology came up first. She clicked on

it.

Bartzebel, it said, was the demon of Mars. There was an ancient artistic interpretation of him with a bald head and ponytail. He had large, bat-like wings and was said to be the demon of storms. Laura moved on to the next name, Elelogap. The same website informed her this demon controlled the elements—particularly water. The next demon was the powerful one, Mersilde—the master of astral projection, who could appear anywhere it desired. Lastly, she looked up Astaroth, the name she'd heard twice. Astaroth, it read—also called Ashtaroth, Astarot and Asteroth in demonology—was the true Crowned Prince of Hell.

Laura put her head in her hands. She longed for her sweet Mia and the warm understanding of her arms. Mia wouldn't judge her. Laura would feel safe divulging everything she feared was terribly true.

"We offer this *virgin sacrifice*," Nana said on the recording. "We offer her flesh in your great name."

But Mia was still deployed. Her down time was minimal, so they'd agreed to talk only when Mia was able to call. This left most of their communication to email, and Laura couldn't possibly explain something like this through one. It was hard enough to tell the woman you loved you were the granddaughter of a strange cultist without having to bite your nails waiting for a reply.

•••

She went back into the basement with a flashlight, wishing she had a cross to wear or some garlic or anything else she'd seen in old horror movies. They were just transmissions, but their nature chilled her, and the unexplained electrical currents that had lit up the tube radio only made matters worse. Still, she pressed on down the steps, each of them creaking with menace as she descended into the waiting dark. The earthy smell hit her, somehow more pungent than previous nights, and there was an odd, coppery taste in the back of her throat. She could hear wayward branches smashing into the sides of the house and fat raindrops creating a clamor not unlike the static voice when the radio snapped on.

"Help me!" a woman cried. She sounded young, a girl really.

Her screams were wild, fear leaving her without restraint. With each cry another mad snake of lightning rose up the frame of the radio to climb the walls.

"The chalice!" Nana said.

"Yes, my queen," another woman replied.

"We spill the blood, for his unholy name."

The crying girl's shrieks became earsplitting, and the lightning formed an azure radiance, like moonlight, covering the basement. As it pulsed and flashed, the peach fuzz on Laura's arms stood on end and the hair on her head had peacocked. The lightning fed off the cries of horror, gaining strength, and when they'd absorbed enough a thick bolt formed, carrying smaller ones on its back as it spun into the center of the basement in a blinding tornado. The tube radio thrummed, its dial spinning like a pinwheel in a hurricane as amorphous blobs of electric fuzz spilled out from the bolt to circle the radio. They each looked like images from a static-filled television and gave off the same wavering glow. As they writhed before her, Laura watched them transform into powdery blue silhouettes.

They were the flickering images of people, and they encircled a long slab. Splayed out upon it was a young woman writhing against shackles. The people came into focus, as if they were VHS images being adjusted by tracking. Women in cloaks. Each wore heavy makeup and fake eyelashes. Their bangs were feathered, giving them all an out-of-date appearance. Standing closest to the slab—exceedingly tall in her high-heeled boots—was Nana. She appeared to be in her 30s and was the only one whose hood was off. Atop her head was a pointed crown bejeweled with sapphires. It glistened as the electricity danced upon its spikes like white worms.

"Rise up, oh powers that be," Nana chanted. "In the name of Bartzebel, I call."

She put her palms up and one of the other women came forward with a dagger. Its blade was curved, the handle made from the head of a petrified snake.

Nana bared her teeth. "Drink of this virgin blood, eat of this virgin flesh. Take this offering, so thee may grant me the sorcery of wind, rain, and lightning."

"Hail! Hail! Hail!"

She raised the blade in both hands and the girl on the slab let out a guttural screech.

Laura winced. *Please, no.*

As the blade entered the girl's breast, Laura joined her in screaming and moved backward, tripping over one of the boxes. Her flashlight spun away but there was no need for it; the hellish blue light had become overpowering, revealing all the horrors of the basement. Dread and revulsion paralyzed Laura. She sat there, watching as Nana sawed the girl's chest open, then her stomach, and then slit her open all the way down to her vagina while she was still alive. Blood gushed purple and the cabal of women moved in hungrily. Nana handed the first one a chalice and she stepped up to the still quivering girl, dipped the chalice into her gaping wound, and brought it back up, dripping. She took a long sip and handed it to the next in line.

Once they'd finished, Nana turned toward the far wall.

"*Introibo ad alatare Satanas.*"

The rest of the coven chanted it back.

Her cabal followed in single file, chiming the bells that were belted around their waists. The one bringing up the rear, who looked no older than fifteen, carried a chain censer that omitted an alluring perfume on tufts of smoke.

My God, I can smell that.

Nana reached up as if touching something on the wall, then stepped into the concrete, letting the wall absorb her. The others followed, each of them vanishing into it. The image of the slab and the butchered girl began to pop and fizz, making sounds like a sparkler as they faded into nothing. The electric cyclone hushed and funneled into the ceiling, the blue light ebbing, and the glow of the radio's dial hummed as all went still, leaving Laura alone in the subterranean darkness below the house.

•••

It's an illusion, she told herself. *It can't be my Nana, it just can't.*

Memories of her grandmother filled her mind: Nana combing her hair when she was a child, coaching her through life, teaching her to drive and dance, sending her off to prom in an expensive dress, and baking her cakes for every birthday.

There's no way Nana would have killed somebody.

She knew something was being projected. She couldn't have imagined that. It wasn't like she took drugs and she had no history of mental illness the way her mother did. Certainly *something* had happened. But Laura didn't trust those images.

Something has taken on Nana's face to mess with me. Maybe this house is haunted or possessed.

But there were the whips and chains she'd found. They were no illusion. And there were still more woolsacks.

Only one way to know the truth.

She got the flashlight off the floor, slid one of the sacks forward, and opened it. She reached in and winced when she touched something sharp. She sucked the blood from her cut fingers and then put her hand back in the sack cautiously. Feeling the blade, she reached lower and grabbed hold of the handle. Bringing it up, her heart sank, already knowing what it would be.

The dagger was long, had a curved blade, and a snake's head for a handle.

As she brought it up in front of her, the radio came alive and more of the blue light shot out of the dial, this time working into a single beam to illuminate the rear wall, the same one the cabal of ghosts had seeped through moments ago. Laura looked back at the bag, seeing a chalice, more daggers, handcuffs, and gimp masks with zippered eyes and mouths. She dropped the dagger and walked to the wall. She touched it, wondering what the significance was. Suddenly she recalled how Nana had touched something before they'd moved on, and Laura began to rub her hand along the top left corner . . .

Her hand landed on a jutting rock.

When she applied pressure it sunk into the wall.

A grinding noise rose up and the wall began to slide to the right. Gears turned and dust fell. She stepped back, her breath getting caught in her chest. As the wall came all the way open the radio's light shone into the hallway lying behind it. The corridor was lined with old torches and each of them came on in unison, their baby blue flames lapping like tongues.

Laura stepped forward.

She was mindful of each step she took, half expecting a trap door to send her screaming into a pit of spikes. Roots had broken through the cracked cement and the air was filled with the smell of decay. The static-filled droning had returned, but this time it had a musical sound to it, like a distorted pipe organ holding a chord. Soon she could see the end of the tunnel, and as she made her way to its lip she saw the large open area, which served as the temple throne.

The ceiling was much higher here—impossibly high for being below the earth—and the floor was clear of roots and cracks, the entire room seemingly immune to the sub layer's general wear and tear. On the wall straight ahead was a giant mural made of black marble. Expertly worked into it were thousands of red tiles forming one huge pentagram, and inside each tile were more symbols and what appeared to be complex mathematical equations, all carved in black like hieroglyphics. Below this motif was another slab; only this one was in the shape of a crucifix, though it lay flat. At each point, metal shackles had been bolted in. The walls were lined with inverted crosses tipped with large spikes, all of which held the telltale stains of old blood. Between the crosses were mirrors of black glass.

Thunder boomed over the thrum. Laura glanced up to see lightning dancing, and when she looked back the crosses were full. Static-blue men and women hung on them, crucified upside down. Their bodies were covered with cuts and sores and black blood poured from their hollowed-out eye sockets.

Laura gasped, recognizing one of them as her grandfather.

They'd left his goofy glasses on even though he could no longer see.

She screamed and all of the hanging bodies joined her, but their screams came out of their mouths in a sound like radio stations being rapidly scanned. Laura backed up, gasping as more blobs formed around the altar and turned into the cabal, Nana once again at the head. Now there was another young woman shackled to the horizontal slab crucifix of the altar and Laura was close enough to see her face.

Laura moaned. "Mom?"

Her mother's head was at the top of the cross, her arms out and chained, and her legs were stretched wide with leather ropes held taut by two of the cloaked women. She was nude and looked no older than eighteen. Tears burned down her cheeks.

Nana addressed her coven.

"We stand before the bloody field of nether, ready to carve and travel from universe to universe."

"Hail!"

"Sanctus Satanas. Dominus Diabolus Sabbaoth."

"Hail Astaroth!"

Her mother writhed against her confines. Laura tried to reach for her but her hands slipped right through, making her image ripple like a pond hit with a stone.

"Bring forth the carriers," Nana said.

On either side of the throne the black mirrors opened. Out of each came a man, each wearing masks made out of the hollowed-out heads of goats, wolves, bears and bulls. They were so freshly scooped of their innards they still bled. With the exception of these ghastly masks, the men were nude, and they moved toward the altar, holding their erections.

"Behold," Nana said. "Six men. Six seeds. For six nights."

"Hail!"

"Behold, my daughter—flesh of my flesh, blood of my blood; innocent, pure and virginal. She is the soil in which we plant our harvest."

Nana turned to the first man and motioned him toward the slab. She dipped her hand into a bowl and sprinkled the white contents all about her daughter.

"With this salt I seal in the power of our master."

One of the other women rang a bell and the young girl began spinning her chain censer, letting smoke tumble down over Laura's mother's face and breasts.

"Rise," Nana said, and the first man climbed onto the cross and lay on top of Laura's mother.

The women with the ropes spread her mom's legs farther apart, the whole coven watching with unflinching eyes as the man arched his back and entered her. His horns rose up triumphantly with each forceful thrust.

"*Satanas – venire!*" cried the women. "*Satanas – venire!*"

"*Veni,*" Nana said. "*Omnipotens aeterne diabolus!*"

"Come, almighty eternal demon!"

Laura dropped her flashlight and turned away from her young mother's rape, tears clouding her vision. After so many painful years, now she knew why Mom had been such a basket case. Sadness reached into Laura's chest and tightened like a fist.

The rapist howled, climaxing, and the room came alive with cheers. Bells rang, finger symbols chimed, and Nana came up with a dagger in each hand and clanked them together. The man climbed off Laura's mother and the next one came forward, excitedly groping himself.

"She is the fifth daughter in the bloodline," Nana said, "and tonight we conceive the sixth and final daughter, my granddaughter, and she will be *the portal!*"

Laura screamed. "No!"

Lightning made the images of the cabal disappear but the blue light and droning noise continued. The walls transformed, looking like dead air on a television, and in the center of the throne's mighty pentagram the image of the tube radio's dial shone through. Once again its hand was spinning, going faster with each lap of its globe. A crack split the floor in two and the halves began to separate, widening the gap. Laura stepped to the altar to avoid falling as azure flames rose from the crack, spreading across the floor in a blinding fog of light. From below, thousands of screams floated up in harrowing echoes. They were the desperate cries of eons spent in torture and madness, cries and screeches and squeals like animals. Laura cupped her ears. Repetitive chants came from behind the electric fuzz but they were muffled and unintelligible, and the church organ grew piercing while the cracking of the flames became one with the sound of static.

Nana rose from out of the crack, floating. Her cloak sailed, its ends burning the same color of her luminous crown. She was older now—just as old as she'd been lying in her coffin at the wake. Strange symbols and numbers were carved into her cheeks and forehead, her teeth thin and jagged. Her eyes were entirely black and they stared directly at Laura.

Nana had slipped through the fabric of death.

"My granddaughter. The time has come!"

Laura stepped away. "No."

"You cannot deny your destiny—your gnostic legacy."

"You killed Grandpa! You let them rape Mom—your own daughter!"

"So you could be born, and carry the infernal light from beyond our universe! *You* are the sixth daughter in the lineage. *You* are the portal. It is through you the great ones will come and bestow their power upon me through my rebirth!"

"I won't let them!"

"It has already begun . . ."

Laura looked down at the irradiating coils twirling around her legs. Lightning bounced from one hand to the other and heat blossomed inside her chest, quaking her ribs so she could barely breathe. She braced herself against the slab.

Nana's voice was clear. "Rise up, Astaroth."

The droning was so loud the walls shuddered. Laura felt as if her heart may stop at any moment as her body shook, her limbs going numb as the electricity surged through her. She could feel their waves shaking her every bone, the moisture on her body instantly turning to vapor.

"*Veni,*" Nana said. "*Omnipotens aeterne diabolus!*"

Laura screamed static.

"Come!" Nana said. "I am ready for the next stage of life, so thee shall fill my soul with thy invincible power!"

Laura's back arched, her arms swimming backward as her hips jutted out. From her chest came a raging luminescence, filling the temple room with roaming lightning.

Something was forcing its way out of her.

They pushed, the blue forms looking like five meaty worms. But as their girth came forward she realized they were not worms, but long, boneless fingers ending with sharp talons made of live, insectile organisms. One hand emerged first, then another, with more following behind them—giant, inhuman tendrils spilling forth, throbbing light like jellyfish as they opened Laura wider though she felt no pain.

"Yes!" Nana cried. "Yes, rise!"

There was a vacuum in Laura's chest now, one that pulled in not just air, but light. In return, it sent forth a glow tinted with colors Laura had never seen. But she had little time to marvel at them. Her breasts had separated, ribs cracking open like cemetery gates, and her abdomen opened, revealing a deep, blue dimension. Standing before her, Nana's face fell slack and her eyes turned white as she stared into the wormhole inside of her granddaughter.

"The gateway," Nana muttered. "The world behind the world."

Laura gasped as her body shuddered, and a sudden blinding bolt of lightning exited her body and ensnared her grandmother like a lariat, lassoing her and then snaking off into multiple electric grapplers that engulfed her body. Nana cried out from the force of it, and the look of wonder that had been on her face was now stained with horror. And what she saw, Laura also saw. It was not so much an image, but an epiphany. Visions raked Laura's mind, flooding her with pitch-black revelations.

Hell was not a place, but an understanding; an understanding that all of humanity was already there. Laura knew now the fingers that tore her open exposed a universe that was a reflection of her own world without all the decoration. This other world was the darkness at the base of the human heart, a place where all life had been born. The long fingers that opened the gate were not defiant of God—they *were* gods. And humankind was not their prized creation. It was one of their amateur efforts, a flawed first draft left abandoned in space and time, left to rot without meaning or purpose. In this sense, these gods were indeed demons, ones so strange and foreign they were beyond understanding.

Nana convulsed, her jowls quivering as blood came blasting from her nostrils. Looking into the void, a crippling terror fell over her. She dropped to her knees. The demons hollered out strange, wordless utterances, and their spindly arms came through Laura like a nest of serpents. Their talons tore deep into Nana, the insects chewing, shredding away parts of her cloak as they pierced her flesh. She opened her mouth to scream, but all that came out was a fountain of blue static. Lightning was cooking her from the inside out, and her eyes burst as a clawed hand wrapped around her skull, scalping her as it forced her down into the sea of greedy fists.

This was the death beyond death, Laura's epiphany told her, but though she wished for it, this was not her grandmother's ultimate end. The things beyond told Laura it was the next phase in Nana's quest for power.

The demons dragged Nana's charred and twitching body back into the void, back into Laura, and she could feel a tight pinching in her organs. She looked away, trying to deny it all, and saw the dial on the wall was beginning to slow and the lightning was retracing into it. She shut her eyes, biting her lips against the pain in her innards, and when she opened them again the static on the walls had faded, the drone fallen to a whisper, and then there was nothing at all. She fell to her knees and reached for her chest, noting she was intact once again, as if nothing had happened.

But it had happened.

She watched the torches on the wall flicker and die and picked up the flashlight just as the temple room went dark. As she moved toward the tunnel she took one look back at the hellish shrine where her grandmother had committed countless atrocities in the name of her dark lords.

Laura's stomach gurgled and she put her hand to it.

Something shifted inside of her.

Laura had to brace herself against the wall. Something was moving within her, and her stomach was swelling and bloating so quickly she could actually see it transforming. And coming from deep within her womb, she could feel little feet kicking.

God, help me.

But the only gods were the very ones who had done this to her.

She tried to run but could only waddle. Entering the hall, Laura found her way back to the basement. She grabbed the lever rock and let the wall slide back into place. Once it was done, she looked back and forth, still hearing a faint crackling. The radio had just the faintest blue glow to it and she stepped forward, listening to the soft noise it emitted. She heard a beating heart, and behind that sound, behind the static, she heard her baby cooing.

DOG YEARS

LAST SPRING THERE WERE ONLY three graves in our backyard.

Mom and Dad were buried side by side beneath the tallest sycamore and Pete, who was Bobby and Julie's cousin, was placed closer to the house so Julie could visit the grave without getting too close to the fence. She liked to make wreaths for the dead from time to time by gathering dead brush. Being twelve, she was the youngest, and we didn't want her going too far from the house, even if we did have pretty good security. The fence itself was only wood, but Dad had lined the top with razor wire when things had started to get bad, and soon after he started on the booby traps. It all had seemed pretty paranoid to me at the time, but it sure doesn't now.

Back when the poison really started to affect the adults, Dad went into overdrive. He was always the survivalist type though. He was into the NRA and all that kind of stuff. There were always guns and knives in the house. He liked to hunt a lot and would skin his own deer. But on top of that, he stockpiled canned goods, water, and batteries and always had a different kit for any emergency you could imagine. That was *before* all the adults started dropping dead. Once the poison spread, he really went apeshit.

He put bars on the windows and extra locks on all the doors. He bought weird weapons like crossbows and swords because he said they were reusable, and he made Mike and me learn how to use and clean every one of them, including all the pistols and rifles. I was anti-gun then, not like now, and when I would argue with Dad, he'd tell me it didn't matter I was a girl and I couldn't count on men to do everything for me. Suddenly it was Mike and me who had to clean all the game and gut all the fish. He made us learn first aid and had us study the U.S. Army Survival Guide. He stocked up on lighters, toilet paper, soap, vitamins, peroxide, charcoal, and canning supplies. His most paranoid fantasy was coming true, and he knew it, even if all of us thought he was overreacting, including Mom, who kept insisting they'd find a cure. But Dad was right in the end, and the proof of it is those two graves beneath the sycamore.

•••

"What do you miss most?" Bobby asks me.

He does this a lot. Bobby's the sentimental type. I've always said he has the heart of a poet. Hell, that was why I'd fallen for him in the first place, back when all we'd had to worry about was curfews and math tests.

"I miss music," I say.

All the phones and mp3 players are long dead now, but we have my mom's old boombox from the attic and a bunch of her tapes. But there's no radio signal anymore and, of course, no power. We have to use batteries to use it, so we don't do it often. Batteries are for flashlights and other more important things. Music's a luxury. We save it for holidays and birthdays, or at least what we estimate them to be. We've been reusing the same calendar.

"What do *you* miss most?" I ask him.

My head is in his lap, and I'm staring up at the sky, which has fallen to the soft lavender of noon. The atmosphere is still changing in spooky ways.

"I miss my hair," Bobby says.

But he's joking.

Granted, his whole head has turned white, but at least he hasn't lost it yet. It's only natural for him to have gone gray by now. He's seventeen, after all.

"What do you *really* miss?" I ask.

He thinks about it for a while.

"The internet, I think," he says. "We got so used to having all that information right at our fingertips. Can you imagine how useful it all would be now?"

I can. I think about that all the time, like when I'm struggling to repair the house or trying to prepare squirrel meat so it's stripped of parasites and not overcooked. The internet would be a tool for me now, as opposed to the toy it had been back when we'd all had it. It occurs to me then just how much time we all wasted in the old days—with our eyes glued to our phones and most of our communicating done through social media. It was such an artificial way to live.

Bobby takes my hand, and I notice the protruding veins on his. He looks down at me, filling my head with warm memoires of hayrides and dances that happened only two years or so ago, and yet now it seems like nothing more than a girlish fantasy I'd had.

"What else do you miss, Skye?" he asks.

Whenever this topic comes up, we have an unspoken rule about not saying we miss our parents. That's a given, just like our health. We don't talk about how we miss running water, air conditioning, or heat that doesn't rely on fire. We don't mention a good steak, cheese, or ice cream. The point isn't to get depressed. It's just to be nostalgic—to try and recapture some of what we've lost.

"I dunno," I say. "Maybe chapstick."

•••

With Pete dead that left four of us.

Mike was the oldest, but he wasn't in charge anymore because his mind was going. Most people didn't live too far past nineteen, and Mike was almost twenty-one. He was still in fairly good shape and was active, but his mind showed age. Most of the time he seemed to have it together, but he often forgot where he was and what was going on. Sometimes he'd even talk to me like I was Mom.

That left me as the head. It was a responsibility I didn't care for, but it was our family's house after all. Bobby was one year older than me, but he'd be the first one to tell you I was better with guns, traps, stitches, and the like. His dad had been a photographer, not a militia nut, so most of what Bobby knew how to do I had taught him. It only made sense I led the way, but I never bossed Bobby around or anything like that. I always thought of him as a partner, not a sidekick. There was just a dynamic to our group that made everyone turn to me. I was never appointed our leader or anything like that, and frankly, I didn't want to be. Whenever we encountered other gangs, it was always best to have

75

one of the males step forward and do the talking. Almost all gangs had male leaders in the dog years.

We called them that because that's what our lives boiled down to.

The poison made people rapidly age, basically at the same rate as a dog: seven years of age for every calendar year that goes by. When it first spread, the elderly just crumbled like dust, and everyone our parents' age started to wither away. It didn't take but a few months for my parents to mirror my grandparents.

It was weird though.

The poison would rot your organs, so you'd deteriorate, but it didn't make you age like normal. Your bones would stay strong because they're not old and your skin wouldn't wrinkle and sag because it hadn't had enough time to. But your eyes would get milky with cataracts, your hearing would fade, your breathing would fall short, and for whatever reason, your hair would go ghost white or it would fall out altogether. Then your organs would start to go and soon enough you'd just go toxic and shut down.

There were other effects of the poison too, such as the girls never menstruating. Before you'd be old enough to have sexual desires, you would've already hit menopause. If you were a dude, you'd be shooting blanks. That was a particularly grim effect because it spelled the end of the human race. The babies born before the poison were going to be the last ones on earth, and they would last less than a quarter of a century.

•••

I go inside to check on Julie and see she's still sitting on the couch where we left her. She's drawing more of her pictures—illustrations she wants to put into a time capsule along with her journal entries, just in case mankind springs anew and wants to know what we were like. I don't have the heart to tell her how unlikely that will be or that all her pictures will have rotted and vaporized by the time new life could form.

Napping beside her is our dog, Teddy. He opens his eyes at the sound of my voice and his tail gets to thumping.

"Where's Mike?" I ask her.

"Upstairs, resting."

My big brother does that a lot these days.

"It's a nice day outside," I say. "Bobby and I thought we could all have a picnic."

That just means a blanket and a very small portion of food. But it also means taking advantage of the warm weather season, which gets shorter each year.

"Okay," she says and gets off the couch.

She goes into the kitchen to put our lunches together. Everyone in the group has their own duties. I go to walk outside and Teddy leaps up and comes to me with his tail wagging. For him, nothing much has changed.

Mom and Dad got him for me when I was twelve because I'd been begging for a puppy for years. They'd finally felt I was old enough to handle it. He's four years old now. If you'd told me when I got him that he was going to outlive all of us, I'd have said you were crazy.

•••

Bobby had started to go downhill early, all things considered. He'd always been more prone to illness though, even before the poison. He used to carry an asthma inhaler around, and he took prescription meds for his nasal problems. But once the dog years came, he had to go without it. I know that wasn't what really broke him down though. It was just the poison itself. Not just what it did physically, but also what it did to him emotionally. It just sort of chewed him up inside even more than the rest of us, which was damn plenty, I'll tell you. He tried to hide it from me, from all of us, but I loved him and knew what was in his tired heart.

He was a poet. Sensitivity ran in his family.

He wasn't a high school football hero turned apocalyptic warrior like Mike.

He wanted to see the good in the world.

He just couldn't seem to find it anymore.

•••

When I come out, Bobby's on the porch staring off into the woods. I come up next to him and see he's watching the birds spin and bleat in the bare branches. I step into him, and he throws his arm around me.

"Betcha nobody ever thought we'd live out our golden years together, huh?" he says.

I pat his chest and ask, "How are you feeling?"

He had a rough night last night, coughing and sniffling beside me. He's phlegmy all the time now and hacks up a lot of blood. He always tries to hide it from me, so I don't say anything. What's the point?

"I'm feeling better," he says, but I know he's lying.

I stand there and just let him hold me, knowing it won't last any more than anything else but wishing it could go on so much longer because it's one of the few beautiful things I have left, and definitely the sweetest. It's not fair that he doesn't have good genes like Mike and me. But then, seeing how Mike is at his advanced age, maybe it's better to go young. All I know is I wish it was me that was fading away instead of him. I prefer dying to going on without my Bobby.

"Birds seem happy today," he says.

"Damned poison only affects us humans."

"The change in the sky and trees seemed to throw them off for a while, but I think they're used to it now."

"Yeah. So am I."

"It's nice to see some beauty left in the world."

He leans in and kisses my forehead, letting me know, like he always does, just how special I am to him. While everything and everyone else has changed, Bobby's still the same. He's my Bobby—the same boy who used to skip rocks on the lake when we were in camp, and the same boy who first kissed me on the floor of the roller rink after he'd helped me up. Just like then, when I feel like I have nothing left to hold on to, I just take Bobby's hand and suddenly it all doesn't seem as difficult as it was a moment ago. Somehow it all seems so, so easy.

•••

I felt worse for Mike.

He had bailed us out of so many dangerous situations when everything had first fallen apart. He'd done a lot of killing, and I know it haunted him. He had been not just our leader but also our hero. He'd fended off people who tried to steal our food and weapons. Later, when times got much darker, he kept the gangs away. He wouldn't even think twice, and he was a great shot too. He taught Bobby how to fight, and he taught me to use a rifle even better than I already could. His word was the code we lived by, and he had never steered us wrong.

But once he'd gotten past twenty, even he was well aware he wasn't fit to lead us anymore. He was forgetful. He would often confuse dreams with reality. He would sometimes talk about people and things from the old days as if they still existed. There were moments of lucidity, but with each day they seemed to lessen in duration.

Mike was the last family member I had left. We would care for him to the bitter end, dementia or not. But there was a hollowness to his eyes now that was at best sad and at worst frightening. His eyes had gone black and wild like an animal, so they seemed to look past you, through you—a look that reminded me way too much of how Dad's were in the end.

•••

Julie comes out of the house with a full tray and begins tapping the rain barrel to fill the tall cup of powdered milk. She comes to the ground where we're sitting in the pale light of the sun and stirs the milk into the oats, and then she opens up the single cans of tuna and pinto beans. For dessert, we each get a spoonful of peanut butter. Tea she has made from pine needles fills three cups. Teddy stands beside us the whole time, drooling. There will be no scraps for him, no matter how much Julie wants to sneak him some. He eats his dog food in the morning and at night only. House rules.

"I'm gonna make rabbit stew with the hare Mike shot yesterday," she says.

It had been a good round of hunting in the brush, even if we hadn't spotted any deer. One thing that hasn't faded in my brother is his killer instinct. He's like a damn wolf. He goes all still and stops breathing, and then he loads the crossbow so quietly you'd think he was a ninja.

"Did you bring him a plate?" I ask her.

"Yes, Skye. But he's still sleeping. I left it on his night stand."

The oats get soggy because I try to savor them, but I ain't about to waste a drop. The tuna is an old standby I'm sick of, but I gobble it down too, wishing I could have some more. Funny how I used to be vegetarian. I sure wish you could grow something in this soil. At least we still have plenty of canned vegetables and fruits.

"I think we'll have some peaches tonight too," I say, thinking of them.

There's not much else to look forward to but meals. We play board games and read old books. We sing songs and tell stories. We get a little buzzed on whisky but never too drunk to shoot. Most of all we sit by the fire to stay warm and hope to make it through another night without any trouble.

This must be what it was like in the old west.

•••

I take it back.

Mike wasn't the one I felt worse for. Julie was.

Julie would be barely fifteen and on her own in a few years. Every day, Bobby and I would teach her new things and help her practice the old ones. He was so good with his little sister. Made me sad to think what a good daddy he would've been to our babies. Julie had become a good cook by then—far better than the rest of us. I'd taught her to take down a squirrel at fifty yards, and she and Teddy were a solid duck-hunting duo. She could find water by following animals at night, and she could identify edible nuts like acorns. She could sew clothes and stitch a wound, build a fire and shelter with sticks, mend a fracture and treat a burn, and she knew how to make Teddy attack as well as back off. These were all skills Dad drilled into Mike and I and we passed down to the others.

But what Julie did best was draw and write, so we saved our paper and all writing utensils for her. She became lost in those imaginary worlds, and who could blame her. The end result was always impressive too. She'd come up with short stories about explorers, ghosts, and princesses she'd read to us by firelight, and she'd decorated the house with portraits of each of us, as well as the still life drawings and landscape pieces. My favorites were the ones she did of Teddy.

Her one wish was to have a guitar. She used to take lessons and still has several guidebooks. There's nothing but time for her to learn to play guitar. If any of us had felt it was safe enough to travel into the city anymore, we would have tried to find her one.

•••

The sky is turning red, meaning the afternoon storms will be coming soon. We all hope it will be more rain. Lately it's been mostly heat lightning and hail. Bobby enjoys the show, but I find each one of them scarier than the last. The weather's gone strange. But it ain't storming yet, so we stay outside a little longer. Bobby and I are alone, and he has his hand under my dress. Julie is in the front yard playing Frisbee with Teddy. In so many ways he's become her dog now, and I'm okay with that. He'll be beside her when we're all gone, and that makes me feel a little better about things.

Bobby and I lift up our heads when Teddy starts growling.

He never growls at any of us.

He goes silent around critters because he's a hunter.

We know damn well what his growling means.

●●●

The garage was our storage shed and where we kept our emergency getaway mini-van. Bobby and I had the master bedroom, and Julie and Mike had a bedroom each. We had a kitchen and a living room, and with Pete gone, the dining room had become just a big, empty space. We had two bathrooms, but we relieved ourselves outside and only used the tubs for our monthly baths, recycling the water from person to person, the girls going first and the boys last. The only part of the house that had changed drastically during the dog years was the attic.

It had a low ceiling so you could only crouch or sit. Up there we kept some extra supplies, along with Pete's old mattress. It was laid out facing the wood blinds of the attic's window, which faced the front yard. It was there to keep your elbows comfortable. Propped up before it, with the barrel just poking out of the window, was the semi-automatic rifle with the telescopic sight and the hand guards attached to the front of the receiver.

The attic was our sniper tower.

●●●

I'm headed inside while Bobby is running to the front yard, going for Julie. We both know the drill. Only this is *not* a drill. I can hear the wood of the front gate cracking, and Teddy is barking his head off now. I'm so glad we keep guns on us. Bobby has his .38 and Julie has her .22. I've got my Glock 19, my personal favorite, but that's not the gun I'm going to get behind.

I'm the best shot of the four of us.

By the time I reach the living room, I can see the front door is open, and I hear the trusty shotgun being pumped on the front porch. Mike is awake and he's ready. I glance outside as I head upstairs and see he didn't even waste time putting on clothes.

I listen as I make my way to the attic.

"Best turn back now," Mike warns, his voice full of gravel.

"We just wanna talk to ya," one of them says.

"I let this shotgun do my talkin for me, boy."

I'm wondering if they saw the bear trap before one of them could step in it.

"A storm's comin," another voice says. "We need shelter."

"There's no room at the inn," I hear Bobby say.

I open the attic door, climb up, and fling myself onto the

mattress.

The rifle is always loaded.

I open the window so I can see and put my good eye at the scope. I see three boys at the foot of the driveway, past the gate they've busted open. Two of them look about fourteen and the other one looks about ten. But we all know this trick. Hiding behind the fence are two older, bigger boys; at least seventeen. I can see them just fine and can pop them from here, but I wait. I'm not like my brother. I hate spilling blood when it ain't necessary. But every one of these bastards has a weapon. The boys behind the fence are packing a rifle, and probably more. One of them has something strapped to his back, but I can't tell if it's a sword or rifle or god knows what. The boys inside hold a machete and a lawn mower blade that has been fitted with a handle, and I can see one of them has some sort of weapon in his pants. Even the little kid has a kitchen knife and what looks like a pipe sticking through his belt.

Mike takes a cue from Bobby's biblical reference.

"You boys are gonna learn about the power and the glory in about two seconds," Mike says.

The wind has picked up, and his long, gray hair and beard spin in it, making him look like a crazed, bare-assed wizard. Bobby has tucked Julie behind him, but her gun is in her hand and I'm proud of her for it. Teddy is roaring like he's rabid.

"We're hungry," one says.

"Learn to hunt," Bobby tells them. "There's no food we can spare."

Seeing their ruse isn't working, one of the older boys creeps forward. I see the other one has a revolver, but he's still hiding, so I keep my sights on the one with the rifle.

"There don't need to be no trouble," the rifleman says. "We just think y'all should share."

"We ain't got nothin," Bobby says.

"Well, maybe you ain't got food and water, but I can see you've got a woman behind you."

My blood burns with anger. I want to shoot him now but don't want to set the others off. My group is outnumbered, after all. They don't know about the fifth boy.

"She's just a kid, you bastard," Bobby says.

"Old enough to spread her legs," the pistol packer says.

To my surprise, Bobby shoots first.

•••

"Kill it," Dad had said.

We were standing in the woods in knee high snow. I was numb from the cold and all I wanted to do was go home, but we had found a deer after hours of hunting and there was no way Dad would let us leave until this was finished his way.

"Shoot it now," he whispered.

The deer was about fifteen feet away, slurping at the creek. I had it in my sights, but I was having trouble seeing because of the tears that kept filling my eyes.

"This is a rite of passage, Skye. You have to learn to kill if you're going to survive."

I didn't want to kill anything, especially not an innocent fawn that only wanted a sip of water. My hands had begun to shake.

"Forget about what you'll do for food," Dad said. "What are you gonna do when someone tries to rape you or kill your brother?"

I fired, sending the fawn tumbling into the rocks of the creek bed. The water ran so red you'd have thought it was full of salmon.

•••

A bloodbath unfolds.

Even Teddy gets into it. He lunges at one of the middle-aged boys, grabbing the arm that held the lawnmower blade. The one with the rifle is winged by Bobby's shots, but as he steps up to shoot, Mike blasts him, pumps again, and blasts a second time before the bastard can even hit the ground. The blood spatters against the fence and the yard is soaked in seconds. Mike moves forward while Bobby holds back, firing from the porch as he makes himself into a human shield for his little sister.

The youngest boy tucks behind the older ones, crying instantly. The pistol packer moves from behind the fence to try and surprise everyone. He takes quick shots at Mike just as I take my shot at him. Mike spins as a jet of blood spurts from his shoulder and the shotgun falls. But my bullet lands in the center of the pistol packer's chest, and he hits the ground screaming. By now Teddy has shredded the other boy's throat. It's wide open, and he's bleeding out quickly. His face is so slick with red I can't tell if he's alive or not.

The machete boy actually jumps into the air like a gymnast and comes at Mike with all he's got. The awning blocks my shot but I see Bobby run to Mike's aid. He fires a round, misses, and

83

then he's out of bullets. But Mike's got the lawnmower blade now, and he's raving like the lunatic he has surely become. The boy is faster than Mike, and he manages to block a few swings with the machete and even slices Mike across the chest. But Mike doesn't even seem fazed by this. He swings the blade down like a sledge-hammer, and it bashes through the boy's defense and sinks about seven inches into the spot where the boy's shoulder meets his neck. His cries remind me he's really just a kid. He falls with the blade still in him. Mike takes the machete from him and starts hacking away. Teddy runs in circles around this terrible scene, barking and barking with his fur on end. I can hear Julie scream-ing somewhere, and the little boy at the front of the gate is para-lyzed by his fear.

I think the war is over, but then Mike does something even crazier than the butchering of the one who lies in pieces in the dead grass.

He starts to run toward the little boy, the machete high above his head, glistening with blood. Bobby sees this and chases after him.

"Mike! No! He's just a kid!" he cries.

Mike reaches the little boy, and just as he's about to chop him in two, Bobby tackles him. They tumble to the dirt, and the little boy finally comes to his senses, drops his knife, and runs out the gate and into the street. Mike gets back up before Bobby can, pouncing like a gorilla. Through my sight, I can see the animal look on his face that has frightened me this past year whenever it has come across him. He's under the hold of his madness now and clearly doesn't even know who Bobby is as he comes down with the blade.

My shot echoes in the dusk as the top of my brother's head comes off. He folds like a raggedy doll and hits the ground, finally at peace. Bobby is covered in blood that is not his own, and Julie, seeing the coast is clear, runs to him, brave considering the bru-tality of what she's just seen. Her love for him overrules any other feelings she could have, just like it does for me.

I trot down the stairs and make my way out into the yard. It's all far more ghastly than it looked from the attic. There are sev-ered limbs and guts thrown about like yesterday's trash. Blood is absolutely everywhere and bullets and the break-in have all but ruined the fence. Bobby is shaking when I reach him, and Julie's sobbing into his stomach—the most I have seen from her since her mom died in her arms.

"Are either of you hit?" I ask.

"Huh?" he says.

His hearing had gone bad already, and now he's half deaf from all the gunfire.

"Are you okay?" I ask, louder.

He nods and pulls me in close. The three of us huddle into a hug for a moment and close our eyes against the awfulness all around us.

"Let's get inside," I say.

The rumble of thunder groans above and as I turn to go into the house I see the flash of steel poking out of the gate. I jump on Julie, pushing her to the ground.

"Duck!" I yell to Bobby, but he's too deaf and slow.

The little boy had a gun after all. What I'd thought was just a pipe was a little, one-shot zip gun.

Julie and I scream as Bobby falls to his knees and leans forward, clutching his belly while blood starts to trickle out of his mouth. I've drawn my gun, but I hear the boy's feet running up the street as he vanishes into the shadows of the dark alleys. I brace Bobby and as he falls backward, I see there's an oozing hole in his stomach. He heaves a bit and struggles to speak as the tears pour down my face. Beside me, Julie is a mess. Her face is in her hands and Teddy is beside her, whimpering and trying to comfort her with nuzzling.

"Take care of her," Bobby tells me.

"I will, baby."

He manages to smile, and my mind reels with late night kisses when he would sneak into my room, the Christmas when he saved up his allowance to buy me the necklace, cuddling through the carnival's cheap tunnel of love, and his gentle touch when he took my virginity on that summer night while we watched the fireflies come out.

"Don't you let this break you . . ." he says through the rising blood.

"Oh, Bobby," I cry. "I love you. I love you."

He's the only boyfriend I've ever had or ever will have.

"I love you too, Skye. I always will."

Tears roll down the sides of his face, and he winces from sadness as well as pain. Julie comes closer and collapses into him, and he manages to turn his head and kiss her cheek, leaving a little

85

smudge of blood. He looks up at me, and I lean down and kiss him one more time. Above us, the red smoke has begun to separate and drift away, and now the stars are fading against all that black. There's the beginning of a rainbow forming in the night. We get these now and then. It's like aurora borealis—rippling beams of multicolored light that make our world gorgeous, if just for a little while. Bobby always says it's the only good thing to come out of the dog years. He loves watching them grow stronger and form into a lovely, wavering festival, but this time he's never gonna see it come.

•••

There are five graves in the yard now, and Julie makes them new wreaths every few weeks. Summer's ending quickly, and the cold is getting stronger. In the living room, Julie and I have set up the old bed Bobby and I used to use so we can sleep by the fire. It's better for both of us this way. I hated rolling over and not feeling him there, and Julie doesn't want to sleep alone anymore. She has so many bad dreams. I hope they'll go away in time, just like I hope mine will. They say time heals all wounds, but that's something we don't have a lot of. All we have is a sisterly bond, a good dog, and enough ammo to take down anyone else who comes near our property.

We're celebrating my seventeenth birthday today, and we're treating ourselves to a feast. With our group cut in half, there's a lot more food to go around, so we're eating better, even though we wish we still had the boys to share it with. I've got one of Mom's tapes playing, but Julie says she has a new song for me. As it turns out, what was strapped to that one boy's back was an acoustic guitar. Tonight we're going to use one of the tapes to start recording them to add to her time capsule.

As for the boy and his friends, I did what Mike had always wanted to do. Their bleached skulls are on spikes out front.

THE SOLUTION

SARAH SPIT INTO HER HAND.

Dallas didn't see it, only heard it. Backstage it was dark, only faintly illuminated by the stage lights left on in the auditorium now that the lunch bell had rang. The two teens stayed quiet in case their drama teacher came back into the auditorium early, or possibly other students who wanted to duck out in there like they were.

At least Dallas was worried about getting caught. Sarah was stoic as always, a void of a girl so thin-lipped, pasty, and plain he'd almost turned down the handjob.

"I wanna see it," she told him while they were rehearsing *Macbeth*, a play Dallas—not being particularly interested in the class as it was—found to be flowery drivel.

He'd thought she'd meant his dick, but she'd made it clear now she wasn't interested in his cock, but rather what it produced.

"I want your cum," she told him.

He hardly knew Sarah, but he'd seen her around school, moping on benches, thick dandruff spattering her sweatshirts like a rain of maggots. She always struck him as a goth-kid without the Hot Topic makeover and black hair dye. Her natural russet hair was anarchic, her features washed out against her pallid flesh and her eyebrows so faint she looked as if she didn't have them until you got close, making her look skeletal and freakishly statuesque.

She was petite, and if there were any noteworthy goodies to her body, they were always cloaked by hand-me-down clothes that fit her like garden trash bags.

"I wanna see what you've got," she said. "I'll bet I can jerk it out of you in five minutes flat."

He snorted, offended. "Hey, I last longer than that."

It wasn't a lie. He was no high school Casanova, but he'd gone to bed with two girls and had gotten head from others. Lately he'd hit a dry spell in the pussy department—the girls at school more interested in the meathead football stars and long-haired rebels— but he still wasn't some two-stroke Johnny.

"I'm really good at it," she said.

She said it very matter-of-factly, without any seduction. There was no lust to her, no joy—just a blank girl behaving like an automatic dialer.

He took her up on the offer, looking at it almost as a dare or a bet, and they snuck into the backstage area and hid until class let out. Now she had his erect cock in her hand and was stroking him, using her saliva as lube. She gave him no dirty talk or soft nothings, only the steady butter churn of her twisting wrist.

She hadn't lied. She *was* good at it.

Sarah was standing behind him so she could take him underhanded, a style his body was familiar with from masturbation. Her breath flowed over his shoulder, smelling of Skittles, her small breasts pressed against his back like Nerf foam. She had the entirety of his genitals out of his fly and she grazed his balls with her fingernails. Dallas felt the pre-cum early on. It pooled in his dickhole and Sarah purposely rubbed it with her thumb.

He thought of his thirty-something homeroom teacher with the caramel arms and plump breasts that quivered under her taut blouses like jam. He thought of the popular girls and their panther eyes, the athletic blondelopes of P.E., and the ivory cheerleaders whose blowjobs were the stuff of lucid dreams.

Had it been minutes or just seconds? Dallas lost count as his legs began to shake.

"Give it to me," Sarah whispered.

Her sudden beckoning nudged him past the edge, creating an orgasmic avalanche, and hot ropes of sperm spurted out of him in a tiny geyser. Even in the brown light he could see Sarah using her free hand to form a cup that caught it. When he was done she dropped his inflamed member and stepped away as he tucked it back in. Still there was no smile, no small talk. She came closer to the crack in the door where the sliver of light fell in, holding up her palm to get a closer look. Her other hand played with it, reminding Dallas of the little plastic containers of play slime he'd always nagged his mother to buy him out of the quarter machines at the grocery store. But there was a seriousness to Sarah that offset the goofiness, making her seem even more odd.

"Such volume," she said, and as he stepped closer he saw what she meant. Her cupped hand was running over. Trails of his dick-snot spilled over the side, the waves of a pool after a cannonball. "Good consistency."

"Um, yeah."

He zipped up his fly. Now that the excitement was over he found himself feeling uncomfortable—not ashamed really, but somewhat embarrassed to have partaken in any sort of sexual activity with such a peculiar outcast. Sarah Owen was not the kind of lay a guy bragged about. She wasn't hideous or fat, but she was a wallflower, transparent in her banality. She seemed to know nothing of social graces, let alone the gifts of makeup and fitting clothes. There was a dull sexlessness to her that was not so much androgyny as it was childish asexuality, so Ben and the guys probably wouldn't believe him even if he did feel like bragging. He sighed, feeling as if he'd violated himself somehow.

"Well," he said, "I'm gonna go get some lunch while there's still time."

He walked toward the door but stopped as she raised the cupped goo to sniff it. He looked away in disgust and when he looked back he saw she was lapping at it like a pussycat with a saucer of cream. It was almost enough to make him ask what the hell was wrong with her, but he chose to let it alone.

Why even bother? Just leave.

As he made his way to the door she looked up from her bowl.

"Come by my house after school," she said.

He blinked. "What?"

She held up her slathered fist. "This is very good stuff."

He felt a headache coming on just from talking to her now. "Listen, maybe we shouldn't have . . ."

"Come by around four if you want the real thing."

He blinked again. "The real thing?"

They held each other's gaze and her movie-cyborg stare made his asshole pucker. She noticed his sudden shift.

"What?" she asked. "Don't you like pussy?"

•••

From the edge of the driveway he looked at the yellowed house with its loose shutters and wood-rotted doorframe. The grass was slightly overgrown. That could be due to the June heat, but the gutted El Camino rusting in the driveway told another story. This was *exactly* the sort of home he would have expected her to come from—a lower-middle-class rental with mildew-green porch boards, a decades-old automobile, and a broken TV antenna. Shingles were scattered on the roof like playing cards and from behind the chain-link fence a cat he could not see mewled in either heat or slow death.

"Christ," he said.

He'd meditated on it throughout the rest of the school day, his mind drifting away from his studies as he weighed the pros and cons of banging Sarah Owen. In the end his teenage hormones won, his desire for vaginal sex outweighing his discomfort around the girl he'd be having it with, as well as the potential humiliation of word getting around school. Having no cell phone to text him with—in 2016, for Christ's sake—she'd written down her address for him. She lived close enough he could walk there in just under half an hour. Now he was here, wondering if he'd made a terrible mistake. He put one foot onto the driveway and then retreated. He was about to turn around and head home when the front door opened and a woman filled the frame.

"Well, hello there," she said.

Dallas couldn't help but smile.

The woman was shapely and blonde and her hair framed the heart of her face like a gold-beribboned valentine. She seemed pretty from afar, even if she was older. She wore only a thin, cotton nightgown even though it was midday. Her bare feet scuffed upon the porch as she came forward, the breeze revealing she wore no bra or panties as it pushed the gown against her. He could see a dark triangle—so she wasn't a natural blonde—and her ample breasts bobbed, the fabric exciting the nipples.

"You must be Dallas," she said, grinning.

•••

The house smelled of tobacco and microwave pizza. The blinds were drawn, leaving the house a suburban catacomb, but there was enough light for him to see the stained rug at his feet so he could dodge the clothes, cereal bowls, and matchbox cars scattered like landmines. Across the den an old dial television flickered, a VCR buzzing beneath it, the two machines cranking out a recording of some horror movie, a '70s one judging by the hairstyles and shirt collars. On the screen a cackling man was eviscerating a busty woman with a chainsaw.

Dallas was no prude when it came to horror movies, but the little boy playing on the floor in front of the set soured him. He looked no older than seven. At least he wasn't watching the program. Instead he was playing with a scuffed-up *Masters of the Universe* figure missing an arm and wearing a duct tape diaper to keep the legs on. All about him was a castle made of emptied soup cans. He didn't even give Dallas a glance.

"Welcome to our home," Sarah's mother said.

Now that he'd gotten a closer look at her he realized she was certainly better looking than her daughter. She had dazzling, hazel eyes and lips that actually knew the importance of a good smile. Her hips were wide and she had a little junk in the trunk, but not so much to make her seem fat, just a little thick. The crow's feet and laugh lines on her face did not hide the fact she'd once been beautiful and the afterglow of that beauty remained, only now there was a layer of trashy desperation lurking just beneath her skin like bacon grease. Dallas took her to be anywhere between forty and fifty—certainly old to a high school senior, but not *too* old.

"Thanks, Mrs. Owen."

She batted his arm playfully. "Oh, just call me Barb." He noticed she let her hand linger on his arm a moment, and she leaned in as if to sniff him before stepping back at the sound of a door opening in the hall. "Sarah, honey, your boyfriend is here."

Fuck, is that what Sarah told her? Is that what Sarah thinks we are now?

Now he knew he'd made a mistake, but it was too early to turn around and leave. He had to at least be polite. Sarah came out of the hall still dressed in her black sweater with the chicken on it. Dallas blushed at the sight of the semen stains on the sleeves, wondering if her mother had noticed or knew what they were. A nauseous panic struck him and he clenched his toes and fists so not to tremble.

"Hey," Sarah said.

"Um, hey."

Sarah turned to her mother. "So whadda ya think?"

Dallas's discomfort congealed as Barb circled him like a tender predator, looking him up and down as Sarah watched with open-grave eyes. He looked away, seeing the carnage on the television screen, and thoughts of cannibal clans came to him and he shook them away, telling himself he was being ridiculous.

But why is she sizing me up?

Barb looked at him intently as she spoke to her daughter. "Good stuff?"

"Very good. Heavy but pliable."

Dallas remembered the way Sarah had played with his jizz. Was this what they were talking about? But that was absurd, wasn't it; to think Sarah was telling her own mother what a class-mate's semen had been like after she'd jacked him off?

Barb reached out and grabbed Dallas's crotch.

At first he flinched, thinking she was going to crush his testi-cles for taking advantage of her daughter. But her hand was gen-tle, caressing his cock and making it stir like a snake roused from its nest.

"Size?" she asked, and Dallas wasn't sure who she was talking to now.

Sarah answered. "About average, I'd say. Maybe five inches or so."

"Nice enough, I suppose. I mean it's always good to enjoy it right? But you said his projectile is good?"

Barb kept rubbing his crotch. She was looking in his eyes now, her lips glistening as the tip of her tongue came out. His cock struggled in the confines of his jeans, his nervousness spreading an odd smile across his face like a corpse rictus.

"Cums like a mule," Sarah said.

Barb unzipped his fly and Dallas jumped. The little boy was just on the other side of the room, still playing and ignoring them, but there.

"I get it," Barb said. "*Not here*, right? You don't have to worry about Bobby. But I understand." She took his hand. "Come on."

She led him toward the hallway with Sarah close behind them. Once there she pulled down his fly and freed his swollen cock. His eyes widened when she got down on her knees in front of him and Sarah did the same, mother and daughter with their faces inches from his erection like something out of a preposterous porno.

"Not all the way hard," Sarah said.

"We can fix that," said Barb before burying her face into his groin, swallowing his entire shaft in one swift chug.

Dallas trembled, one knee nearly buckling. He'd never had a girl deep-throat him before. The girls his age were novices and it showed. They lapped at it and only sucked the head, relying on the hand to do most of the work. But Barb was a cocksucking champion, sending his mass to the back of her throat without the slightest gag. When she pulled away, a long strand of saliva hung between her flushed lips and his penis, only falling away when she smiled.

"He's hard now."

The two of them looked at his cock and Barb cupped his nut-sack, staring at it like she was putting deli meat on a scale.

"He's still full," Barb said, "even after your stroke-job."

"He came a lot too. He refills fast."

"Good."

They got up and Barb grabbed his erection and used it to guide him toward the bedroom, Sarah tagging along behind them, Mommy's little helper.

•••

He didn't know why they behaved this way but he wasn't about to question this living fantasy—two girls at once, a mother-daughter duo, one of them a MILF with meaty tits and a bottomless pit of a throat. He did as he was told, stripping nude without another thought.

Barb sat on the bed and Sarah took a folding chair and placed it against the wall.

"She watches," Barb said.

"Huh?"

"While you fuck me, she watches." She pointed to Sarah. "She *only* watches."

He was a little bummed to hear he wasn't going to have his first threesome, but he would much rather bang Barb than Sarah, so he shrugged and agreed. Barb pulled the nightgown up and off of her. Dallas watched her tits sway, admiring the tanned areolae of her pimpled nipples. He scanned the rest of her body, excited by her muscular thighs and hips even if he was a little put-off by the looseness of the flesh around her stomach, which he figured was the high cost of having two kids. But despite this she was still very sexy, her mature body hard and speckled with an array of brown freckles, making him wonder if she sunbathed in the nude in their backyard. She beckoned him with a curling finger.

Once on the bed he made a clumsy move to get on top of her but she flipped him onto his back with a strength that surprised him. She nibbled at his chest, biting the nipples with enough pressure to make him wince, and then her head sunk lower and she inhaled the reek of his crotch, a stink of dried semen, her daughter's spit, and his own sweat, a swampy mélange birthed by the humid day. Then her mouth went around his cock and she began to milk him, sinking his dick into her head so deep that when she stuck out her tongue it tickled his balls.

All the while Sarah sat there in the corner, a sliver of sunlight stabbing through the blinds to land across one side of her face. In the beam, flurries of dead skin flakes and dust danced in a luminous orgy.

Barb released him from her jaws and climbed him, bypassing his eager cock as she mounted his face like a wanton bull rider. She was already sopping and her tang filled his mouth and nostrils as she nearly suffocated him with her flushed pussy lips. She rocked back and forth and started fucking his face. It was something he'd never experienced before so he just went on instinct, spinning his tongue inside of her pulsing canal like a burrowing worm and clutching her buttocks. Barb made a strange clucking sound and began to whinny like a horse. She made several feral noises in her mad estrus, a barnyard bitch braying at the moon. She rocked him against the box springs so hard he felt like he might get whiplash, but he was thunderstruck by sexual hysteria and wanted nothing more than to surrender his body to her and let her devour him with the voraciousness of a mother wolverine. He felt her vulva pulsate and he took pride in it, knowing he was doing something right, and when she suddenly came, a jet of fluid burst from the anterior wall of her hole, flooding his mouth with salty froth of female ejaculate that sprung from her Skene's glands.

Barb pounced on him and took his still rock-hard dick and guided him into her vagina. She began to ride him, shaking the entire bed as she grabbed the headboard, her mighty tits flapping about like beached salmon.

Sarah sat on her chair, watching, her eyes pools of black rain.

"Oh God," Dallas cried, feeling the semen rising inside of him.

"Give it to me," Barb said. "Gimme that cum."

It came in a squall. He was almost surprised the burst didn't knock her off balance. It was like a stream raging in the electricity before a thunderstorm. Barb didn't pull him out, didn't break stride. She actually clenched her pussy, milking him with added pressure as she squealed and spun like a giant golden-crowned flying fox.

When he was done she immediately slid off him and tucked her hand under her pussy, and he watched as her daughter came forward with something glass in her hands and helped Barb affix it. He saw Barb's abdominal muscles contract and her vaginal lips came open, letting his semen sluice from out of her as Sarah collected it in a small mason jar.

•••

They told him to keep quiet and return the next day, four o'clock sharp, so that's what he did. He would do nothing to rock this love boat. He'd never been so gloriously fucked and fellated. Barb was more than a mere woman, he decided. She was a ravenous sex goddess, a libidinous Madonna singing *come-hither* from the pink tunnel between her spread thighs.

When he'd left, Dallas felt like he'd been in a car crash, struck with post-coital ataxia. She'd drained his scrotum so completely the walk home was a drunken one and once he got there he went straight to his bedroom, telling his parents he had an upset stomach so he could skip dinner. He lay in bed, exhausted but unable to sleep as visions of sweaty female bits slapped his mind.

The only thing that irked him was the collecting of the sperm. It left a shit-stain on the otherwise glorious escapades. It was just so raw in its queerness. What was the purpose of it? Was it some sort of souvenir? Was it an experiment—Sarah keeping it under a black light as some kind of science-fair demonstration? Why the obsession over velocity and weight? Why an interest in the fucking semen at all? The other girls he'd had sex with seemed all too eager to get as far away from it as they could, telling him to pull out and only letting him cum on their bellies. When he'd cum in Jenny Slade's mouth last winter she'd turned away from him and vomited the white mess in the grass. So if other girls treated his spunk like acid rain, why did the Owen women find it so fascinating?

Upon leaving he'd passed by the little boy lying on the floor. The kid had a Popsicle in his hand, running sticky red down to his elbow. He was staring at the television and Dallas's heart had skipped at what he saw on the screen. The horror movie was off, the tape replaced by some sort of medical documentary. A mortician was standing over a carcass on a slab. The top of the corpse's head had been sawed off and the mortician was scooping out the brain with his hands, cupping the bloody, gray mass much as Sarah had cupped Dallas's sperm. The boy watched the screen, sucking on his Popsicle, his legs kicking absentmindedly like a schoolgirl writing in her diary, watching like he'd seen it a hundred times.

Also on his way out, Dallas noticed a few framed photographs on the wall he'd been too distracted to notice before. They were pictures of the whole family, including a strong-jawed man with stringy hair who could only be Mr. Owen. Dallas picked up the pace on his way out.

So she's married, so what?

Or was she? She might have been widowed or divorced. Did it really matter? It would be odd for a daughter to betray her father by getting her mother some stranger on the side, but Sarah and Barb's relationship was clearly fucked up anyway, so what difference did that make? As long as the guy was at work at four o'clock Dallas honestly didn't have a problem. He wasn't going to stop crushing pussy that sweet just because there was a ring on the finger attached to it.

All day at school he struggled against the urge to tell some of the guys what had happened to him. It was torture hanging out with Ben and Cody without telling them about his monumental fuck. But he remembered what Barb had told him.

"You tell anyone and it's bye-bye," she'd said, pushing her breasts together and arching her hips forward so her vagina winked at him.

When the final bell rang he nearly catapulted out of his seat. He walked fast, so eager he arrived a little bit early. His phone said 3:40. But did twenty minutes really matter? His semi-hard cock pressed against his Levi's, assuring him it didn't.

As he came upon the house he saw the front door open. He thought Barb or Sarah had seen him coming, so he picked up his pace again only to see a man coming out of the house. Fearing it was Mr. Owen, Dallas scrambled to get behind a bush and ducked down low. But when he looked through the leaves he could see that it was not Mr. Owen at all. In fact, it wasn't a man, at least not an adult one.

It was another boy of about eighteen years of age.

Barb gave him a long kiss goodbye and patted his ass as he

walked off.

•••

They're running a train station, Dallas thought bitterly.

He was partly jealous (because he'd thought he'd been special—sure, not romantically, but special nonetheless) and partly just shocked.

They're running a goddamned train on that pussy. I've been tapping municipal cock-wash.

This disturbed him but he didn't turn around and go home. His aching balls wouldn't allow it. All day long he'd made them promises and if he didn't pay up they'd turn on him in the night, turning blue as plums and nearly as large. So once the other boy was out of sight, he left the bushes and headed toward the Owen house. Today there was a series of discarded Natty Ice cans scattered across the lawn like busted gnomes.

Must have been a wait.

Sarah welcomed him inside with her usual apathy. When Dallas saw the young boy watching TV he was sadly not surprised to see it was an Asian fetish film featuring a virginal young woman being attacked by a squid on a subway. The rubber tentacles lifted her skirt and pinched at her rosebud breasts. The boy was wearing only a pair of Batman undies and a ski mask, and he was clinking a pair of spoons together over a bowl of ravioli that had dried to crust.

Today the house smelled not only of cigarettes and junk food. There was a stench that lurked beneath it, something foul like rotting sweet potatoes or trapped rodents. Sarah led him down the hallway and into the bedroom where Barb stood in another gown. This one was purple and lacey, much more sensual than the one she'd had on the day before. Her cheeks were flushed, her hair a tornado of bleach.

"And how's my fuck machine today?" she asked.

He tried to hide his sourness. "Good, I guess."

"Something wrong, baby?"

He almost came out with it, almost demanded to know what the hell was going on, but he was too afraid—afraid to lose easy pussy this good and afraid he'd learn more than he wanted to know about these women. There was a demented chaos to this family, one that was becoming more and more apparent to him. Inside the Owen's house he felt like he was moving through a layer of silt and feces, as if madness itself was quarantined between these peeling walls.

Barb came closer, turned around, and lifted the hem of her nightgown. Her hefty, bare ass grazed across his bulge, the cheeks tightening and relaxing again and again in an anal kiss. He put his arms under the gown to cup her breasts, feeling the sweat on her body and smelling the cum on her breath.

Flames flooded his blood and he pushed Barb to the mattress and bent her over. She gasped in delight. Dallas didn't bother undressing and he didn't bother with foreplay. He didn't need to spit in his hand. She was already drenched. He was rock hard as he plunged into her and she cried out in a way that made Sarah stand up. Barb smiled to let her know it was okay, and Sarah returned to her seat as Barb began to cluck like a hen. As he thrust harder her clucks became the morning cock-a-doodle-doo of a rooster and her legs kicked like a strutting chicken beneath him.

He flipped her over and pushed her to her knees before the bed, a little too excited when he shoved his dick in her mouth. He felt something hard slide around in her mouth with him and Barb pulled away, his cock tugging her dentures from her lips. The false teeth hit his sneakers. It wasn't a simple bridge to replace a few missing teeth. These were full, complete dentures. Dallas grimaced. Barb looked up at him with her lips curled into the black hole of her mouth, aging her.

"Circulation problem," she said, her words slightly garbled. "They all fell out."

Dallas didn't know what to say. His cock began to deflate, a popped birthday balloon.

"Need some more lead in your zeppelin," Barb said, and her eyes grew crazy. "Ever had *a gummer?*"

"A what?"

But then he knew as she put his cock back into her mouth, sans dentures. Without teeth she could clench his cock with her gums, applying incredible pressure. Dallas was rattled by discombobulation once again as she pumped him, her hair fluttering as her head shook like a jackhammer, her clenched jaws claiming dominion. He fired his jism into her mouth and roared while she moaned and moaned, never stopping, letting his seed fill her skull. He stumbled and was grateful to have Sarah catch him and help him to the chair she'd been sitting in. She went to her mother who had tilted her head back to keep as much of the semen in her mouth as possible as some of it seeped from the corners of her mouth and trickled out of her nostrils. Sarah placed the mason jar under her mother's head and Barb's mouth burst open like a great zit.

"What a load!" Sarah said.

"Oh my god," Barb said as she caught her breath, mascara tears running down both sides of her face. "That was the biggest wad I've ever had in my mouth. Where the hell do you store all that, Dallas?"

He merely shrugged and excused himself to the bathroom.

•••

As he pissed, he looked at the books and magazines stacked on top of the toilet tank; medical magazines, a volume on anatomy, one porno rag and two books that stood out to him—one on Saracen sorcery, the other an encyclopedia of demonology. After cleaning up his soggy crotch he caught himself in the mirror and wasn't too happy with what he saw. Making his way down the hall, he tried to catch the murmurs coming from the bedroom.

"Are you close?" Barb asked her daughter.

"Soon, soon."

"Well," Barb said, sounding disappointed. "I guess you can't force it."

"Soon, Mother."

Force what? Close to what?

He lingered in the hallway a moment but they'd fallen silent. Figuring they knew he was out there he pushed the door open and stepped inside. Sarah was sliding the dresser drawer back in just as he entered the room. Seeing him, Sarah pushed it in quickly, and he pretended not to notice the mason jars that filled it, nor the strips of masking tape on the lids that bore many different names including his own.

•••

"You've got to keep this a secret better than me."

Ben was a tall hipster who'd been Dallas's best friend since the 12th grade, and he sat across from him now, smiling and waiting for Dallas to say more. Dallas had been itching to tell someone despite the risk of doing so. Now it wasn't just because he wanted to brag about his prowess; it was because everything had spiraled. If not advice, he at least needed solace.

"What is it, man?" Ben asked. "You've been acting weird all week."

He'd been back there four more times and each time had been more intense than the last. Every time he showed up the bed was tossed and her pussy was already sopping. Every time he came—whether in her mouth, vagina, or even one time in her anus—the semen was squeezed out and encapsulated in the little jars like preserves. He knew they were stockpiling, but why? It didn't just bother him. It wasn't just disgusting and weird; it was frightening. When he tried to close his eyes at night he saw the dresser drawer closing, saw his own name amongst several others on the jars.

"Okay," Dallas said, not even sure where to begin.

He decided to just start from the beginning and not bother trying to sugarcoat or leave anything out in the name of pride. But he didn't even get halfway through his story when he noticed his friend's face had paled.

"Ben? What is it?"

Ben shook his head and couldn't keep eye contact. "Shit, man. I've been fucking Barb too."

Dallas felt gravity leave the earth.

"The sick bitches," Ben said. "They keep *my cum*, man! They put it in fucking *jars!*"

•••

It was a muggy Saturday night. Moths fluttered at porch lights like epileptic angels and mosquitoes buzzed in the ears of prey. The street seemed longer than it had ever been in the daylight and yet the house came upon them quickly, as if it knew they had no idea what to do when they got there.

Ben was clearly having second thoughts.

"Fuck this, man. Let's get outta here."

"Come on! Don't you wanna know what they're up to?" Dallas asked. "Don't you want to know why they've been doing all of this?"

"To hell with it, man. So they're a couple of crazy bitches. Let's just wash our hands of them. I'm sure as hell not coming back now, I don't care how good the pussy is."

"You just want to walk away from this?"

"Yeah."

"Without knowing why they're collecting the sperm of half the guys in our senior class?"

"Yeah! I mean, sure it's weird, but what do we care? We got our nut; let them do whatever they want with it. It's just cum, for God's sakes."

"I know that. I'm not saying it's fucking diamonds. I just want to know what the hell they're doing with all of it. I want to know why they lured us here and what Barb really fucked us for."

"'Cause she's a horny, old bitch! Now *let's go.*"

They were close enough now to the Owen house to see the white flickers of a television screen lighting up the window. Dallas didn't even want to think about what little Bobby was watching this time. *Faces of Death*, perhaps?

They had no real plan. They'd just decided to confront the Owen women. They didn't have an appointment and they didn't know if anyone but the usual trio would be there. Dallas had it in his mind that the women would panic and scramble for an explanation, but now he wasn't so sure. Maybe they'd just laugh and find a way to lure he and Ben in for another round. He liked to think not. He'd been blinded by his horniness before, but now the secret nightmares going on inside of the Owen house had teased his curiosity more than his cock, and he was determined to uncover the truth, sticky and vile though it may be.

"So she promised you he was away?" Dallas asked.

He had never asked Barb or Sarah about Mr. Owen, the man in the pictures. He'd been too nervous to bring him up. But Ben had been so nervous that he *had* to ask, and Barb had told him not to worry, that Mr. Owen was away on important business.

"Said he was for weeks," Ben confirmed.

"That he *would be* or that he already *had been*?"

Ben was rattled. "I dunno, man. She just said not to worry, that he wasn't going to be home for a while."

They were at the foot of the driveway now. The house loomed like a haunted sanitarium.

"I'm going up," Dallas said, even though there were so many reasons not to.

Ben hesitated, but he was a good friend and wouldn't allow Dallas to do this on his own. The only light coming from inside was of the shuddering TV, but they heard no sound coming from it. The house was as peaceful as a mausoleum and just as spooky.

Dallas swallowed hard and rang the bell. It echoed through the house and they stepped back, suddenly afraid. They saw no shadow move past the blurred glass on either side, but the door opened on its own. No one was standing in the doorframe. Dallas gasped but then he looked down and saw it wasn't the work of witchcraft and ghosts. It was Bobby who had opened it. Half his body peeked out from behind the door, dressed in a magician's

cape and cheap-looking monster mask. The kid clearly couldn't
see out of it so he slid it up so it rested on top of his head like a
rubbery beret. He didn't say anything, and for the first time Dallas
got a good look at the kid's face. His teeth were rotted the color
of sewage and his eyes possessed the same existential nothingness
of his sister's, only there was a deeper darkness to them, a subterranean dementia caused by being home schooled on morgue videos and cold Chef Boyardee while his mother fucked a steady herd
of neighborhood boys and his sister canned their fresh-squeezed
semen. It dawned on him he had never heard the child speak, and
he wondered now if he was deaf and dumb on top of being dan-
gerously neglected.

They didn't know what to say, and little Bobby didn't bother
with a hello. He just stepped aside to let them in. Immediately
upon entering the house Dallas could sense something was
stranger than usual. The foul stench that had been germinating in
the house was now acrid, a hellish combination of a fish-market
dumpster and a men's room at a sulfur plant. Dallas covered his
face with his t-shirt and Ben gagged.

"Holy shit!"

"Did the toilets back up or something?" Dallas asked to no one
in particular.

Bobby didn't seem fazed by the odor at all. He walked toward
the kitchen and Dallas and Ben followed. Dallas expected to find
the kitchen table still holding a meal from days earlier, covered in
flies, and the sink to be overflowing with dishes. But the sink was
empty and the table was clear. Even the trashcan had been emptied. The house was its usual chaotic mess but there was no garbage to attribute the pungent smell too.

Bobby led them to a door. The kid looked up at them as he
pointed toward the knob.

"They're down there," was all he said.

•••

The basement was cold—freakishly cold given it was nearing
summer. Dallas moved down the staircase gingerly, as if avoiding
bear traps, and behind him Ben walked on his tippy toes. Bobby
left them to return to his videos, closing the door behind him. The
stairs were in a private shaft, separated from the basement itself,
so all they could see was a bronze glow at the foot of them.

There was a murmur—a hard sigh that sounded male.

"Shit," Ben whispered.

He turned back, terrified that Mr. Owen was home, but when he reached for the doorknob, it wouldn't budge. It clicked on its bolts as he tried to turn it, locked.

"Shit!" Ben said again.

Dallas was equally afraid. Beads of sweat formed at his spine and swam down the crack of his ass, his teeth chattering like a typewriter.

There was another moan now, longer and deeper, unquestionably male.

"What're we gonna do?" Ben asked.

But there was only one thing they could do. It was what they'd come here for.

"Come on," Dallas said.

His feet hit raw earth and he looked into the open room, seeing a bare bulb hanging from a single cord. What it lit up made Dallas let out a short cry of horror and he stumbled backward into Ben. When his friend saw it, he screamed like he was ten years younger.

Barb was standing over a metal slab, nude but for a latex apron that mashed her tits together. In her hand was a thin paintbrush she was dipping into one of the sperm-filled mason jars. On the slab before her was a man; only he wasn't a normal man. He was a gray husk, rotted and yet still wiggling, a traveler who had been caught between the land of the living and the land of the dead. Parts of him were badly decomposed, the beef-jerky flesh having flaked away at sections to reveal the saffron of sun-bleached bone. There was a purple goulash where his bowels should have been and the cavity in his broken chest seeped like a diseased vagina belching black blood. He would have been an absolute zombie had it not been for the completely healthy right arm and the smooth perfection of his face. These two parts were like any other normal, living human being's. The eyes flashed, baby blues, and looked right at Dallas, who stood there frozen, recognizing him as Barb brought the brush forward and laid a base of semen on the monster-man's neck.

"Hello, boys," she said, not looking at them.

There was a shuffling in the corner and Dallas noticed Sarah for the first time, squatting beside the table with her pants off. Blood ran down the insides of her legs as she tried to scoop it into a jar and beneath her was a plastic bucket as a safety net, so she wouldn't lose a single drop.

"Hey," Sarah said, as if they'd just bumped into each other in

103

detention.

Dallas couldn't reply. White-hot horror made a noose around his throat.

"Boys," Barb began, "this is my husband, Lyle."

Lyle smiled and waved his good arm and then chuckled at how the two boys remained paralyzed by fear, choked by the sheer abomination of him.

"That's all, Mom," Sarah said.

She stood up and sealed the jar and handed it to her mother, not bothering to put her pants back on. Her bloodstained thighs glistened like expunged tapeworms. Her mother held up the glass jar for inspection.

"It took long enough," Barb said. "But it's a nice, heavy flow. Like I always say, you can't rush a good period, even if you do ovulate all the time."

Barb put the jar down next to the row of sperm-filled ones and dipped the tip of the paintbrush into the reddish-brown swill. She returned the bristles to her husband's neck and painted his flesh over with their daughter's menstrual blood.

"Jesus!" Ben said.

He shrieked and turned back to the staircase but in his panic he stumbled, and as he tried to right himself mid-fall he put all his weight onto one ankle. Dallas winced as he heard it shatter. Now Ben shrieked even louder, his terror and pain making a chorus gurgle in his throat. Dallas wanted to go to his friend, to carry him up the stairs and kick the goddamned door down. But he could not move. He was immobilized at the sight of this monstrosity, with its doting women who baptized it in their harvest of bodily fluids. He watched as each stroke of the brush blended the semen and blood, and how this human puree glistened on Lyle's dead flesh, moisturizing it, turning it from black to brown and then to a newborn pink as fetid pus oozed around the edges and old skin shavings rose from the body in bloats of smoke.

Dallas was reminded of the time-lapse films he'd seen in biology class, which showed fruits and dead animals decomposing at a rapid rate. This was what he was seeing here, only in real time and in reverse. The slurry of sperm and blood was like fuel to Lyle's body. It was reforming his badly damaged carrion in small, spurting fragments—the antithesis of decay. It was as if he was being born again out of his own waste, a grown-man fetus rising from the black mess of his own gore.

"He's responded so well to your sperm, Dallas," Barb said. "Every drop helps, but you give twice the bang for my buck as the other boys."

"What is this?" Dallas said.

"You're in the chamber of creation," Sarah said. "We're bringing Daddy back to life."

Barb smiled at him, the same seductive snarl that had lured him to the mattress. "Life isn't just a linear dash to the finish line." She plucked a drop of semen on one fingertip and dabbed another in blood. "The tools of life are ours—the seed in one hand, the egg in the other."

"What?"

"Sarah is rather unique. She's always ovulating, you see. Her menstrual blood isn't just the usual waste regular women produce. She releases fertile eggs to go with all of this semen you boys are all too happy to give up." She winked. "Not that I don't enjoy taking it from you. But of course you knew I was a nymphomaniac, didn't you?"

"But . . . what is this . . ." Dallas couldn't find words.

"It's simple. There's birth and then there's *rebirth*."

"But he's dead!"

"Not anymore. Death is malleable when you have the tools of life. My husband has passed through death and back. That was his dream. That's what he worked and studied for. Now he's more than human."

She dabbed her husband behind his ears with the fluids and he made a mewling sound much like the cat Dallas thought he'd heard on his first visit. Barb smiled and clucked at him. Sarah joined them by bleating and scratching her feet in the dirt like a dog covering its own excrement.

"You're all insane!" Dallas stepped back and bumped into Ben, who was now passed out at the foot of the stairs. "You're fucking insane!"

Barb's face turned serious. "There's nothing crazy about a family sticking together."

Sarah fumbled with something on the table and then charged him. He made for the stairs but she tagged his leg with a taser. Yellow knives of fire shredded his tendons and nerve endings, sending him to the floor in a twitching heap. Before he could regain control of his limbs she reached for a toolbox and wrapped a small length of chain around his hands and locked him to the

105

banister.

"Soon Daddy will be all better," she said. "I've been *saving myself* for him, like a good girl. Keeping my eggs coming, keeping myself pure—all for him."

"Yes, you are a good girl, sweetie," Barb told her. "You'll feel Daddy's touch soon enough. But right now, step back so Daddy can do what he needs to do."

Sarah's eyes brightened, making her look more alive than Dallas had ever seen her. She smiled wide and her cheeks flushed with color, a child on Christmas morning.

"You mean . . . he's gonna . . . ?"

She couldn't even finish. She was too excited.

"What?" Dallas asked. "What's going on?"

Barb motioned to her daughter and Sarah skipped over.

"Elevate him," Barb said.

Sarah put her hands on a long pole jutting from under the table where the man lay. She pumped it up and down like a car jack, and the table folded upward on a vertical slant. Dallas twitched as Barb approached him, but she passed him over and went to Ben, who was just beginning to stir. She stripped Ben of his shirt, then undid his shoes and pulled off his pants. She then slid her hands under his armpits and hoisted him up.

Ben groaned. "What's going . . . on? Where . . . where am I?"

Barb stood him right before the edge of the table and held him up. The slab was now at an angle that made Lyle's head nearly level with Ben's. Dallas saw the man's smile transform into a horrible grimace. While his face looked normal and alive, it was incomplete, unstable, for when it moved the folds of flesh slid upon the skull like melted cheese, still staying in place but slithering with uncertainty. His cheeks were slick with semen, his lips worms of menstrual blood.

Ben came to his senses just in time to see the creature's jaw unhinge, his skull popping open like a Pez dispenser, releasing a long tongue that unfurled like manure. Ben screamed and Lyle's mouth released a horrible zoo symphony—mewling coyotes, mating gorillas, and dying lionesses crying to heaven from hell. Dallas could feel the vacuum Lyle's mouth made, but it was a strange vacuum that did not pull wind but rather energy, like a magnet. But he could also tell he was only feeling the residual effects. This roaring vacuum was intended for Ben.

In horror, Dallas watched as Ben's flesh began to glisten with red sweat. Tiny drops of blood appeared all over his body, pushing out from every pore. He was not being cut, not bleeding in the normal way. He had no wounds. The blood was being *pulled* out of him through his skin, his body being wrung out like a soiled rag. As the roar intensified so did the vacuum's pull. Ben's body jerked as his blood left him in a horizontal rain and soon he was a hydrant of gore, his screams joining the chorus of animal howls as every last drop he had flew into the churning black hole of Lyle's mouth.

Barb let the spent body fall with a wet thud. Ben fell into a fetal position in death, a dumpster-bound abortion. Dallas turned away from the sight and was grateful for the tears that blinded him. He didn't open his eyes until he felt someone patting his head.

"There, there," Barb said. "Don't cry."

Through the tears he could see her face smiling down at him like a breast-feeding mother.

"Yeah, Dallas," Sarah said. "He's full now. Besides, we wouldn't let him feed on *you.*"

Dallas blinked away his tears with panicked eyes.

"I'm sure your blood is very nice," Barb said. "But it just can't compare with that incredible cum of yours."

He flinched as she came closer, but his hands were locked behind him so he couldn't bat her away when she reached for his belt buckle.

"There's still a lot of life needed," Barb said. "We've got a lot of work to do." She pulled his cock out of his pants and started to stroke it, her fingers slick with Ben's blood. "But now that you'll be staying with us, we'll have plenty of time to work . . . *and play.*"

Dallas heard Lyle gurgle and when he looked over at the man-beast he saw the stew of his innards stirring, awakened by the eight pints of blood he'd devoured. A hose of white intestine writhed from out of the chum, rising like a cobra, belching runny fecal venom from its spout.

Barb touched Dallas's chin, turning him back to her.

Her face was flattered by the soft lighting smoothing her wrinkles and casting sweet shadows over her eyes, making her look youthful and innocent although she was neither. She was as lovely as she was mad—such beautiful wreckage—a ballerina being ravaged from the inside by a school of piranha. She arched her back and undid the apron, unleashing her breasts. Her blonde locks spun across them. She gave him a smile. Then she reached in and removed the smile, placing her dentures on top of the blood-slick apron.

To his shock and revulsion, he felt himself getting hard.

"You teenage boys," Barb said. "Nothing stops you."

As her gums closed around him, he knew she was right.

SKYSCRAPER

ALL THEY COULD DO WAS scream.

It didn't even look like water anymore. Wood and metal from shattered buildings filled the churning waves, transforming them into a surging mass of garbage. The boat stayed upright as Stan clung to the railing, but the flooded streets swarmed with floating vehicles slamming into each other like bumper cars before being swallowed whole. As the waves had rushed over the walls surrounding the town, homes and small business were lifted from the earth and sent drifting as if they were no more than dead leaves.

Survival was all that raced through Stan Trotter's mind. There was no time to mourn the loss of everything. The fishing boat they were on, which had been turned into an emergency lifeboat as the storm had intensified, seesawed on the rough waters, threatening to capsize. The packed crowd shrieked. Tara clung to Stan with a might beyond her four years.

"It's okay, honey," he said.

But nothing was okay. There weren't enough life jackets to go around and everyone was standing on the open deck, clinging with white-knuckled fists. The rain was gray and merciless, the wind pushing it in every direction. Stan was soaked beneath his poncho, and the cold was cruel. He could only imagine how his daughter felt.

"Please, God!" Tara sobbed. "Please save us."

It was her mother who'd filled the girl with religion. Kate always leaned toward Christianity, though she rarely went to church. Stan had been against bringing their daughter up to follow any religion, but now that they were staring down the very real possibility of mass death, he was glad his little girl had some sort of higher power to trust in. If nothing else, it would make her feel closer to her mother in this bleak moment. Stan wondered where Kate might be, if she were safe somewhere in the dystopia their world had become. They'd been divorced for three years, but that didn't mean he'd stopped caring about her. He doubted he ever would.

Ignoring Tara's prayers, the storm intensified, deafening Stan. In the distance he saw clouds twisting—the same strange, undulating clouds that had come at the start of this waking nightmare. They moved far faster than any he'd seen before, as if he were watching a time-lapse video.

"Daddy!" Tara sobbed in his ear. "I want to go home!"

But there was no home. Their house had been pulled from its foundation and sailed into the tsunami like the rest of their neighborhood. *What good is buying a generator and stocking your garage with canned food if your house is just going to float away?* He'd seen this disaster coming weeks in advance, but his team had been unable to convince Banacheck and the council to listen to their predictions, even though Stan had been one of the chief designers of the Weather Plexors.

The entire west coast of America was drowning as a result.

•••

"This could cause an even greater disaster than the drought," Stan had told Mr. Banacheck, the head of the fund. "We need to do test runs, in small increments, then build up to a full sequence."

Banacheck shook his head. "What you're suggesting would cost our silent partner an exorbitant amount of money. They've already covered the high cost of thousands of lasers and the mothership to carry the aerosol-filled sails. You're millions over budget as it is."

"We need those lasers so they can combine to form the phased array laser—"

"To give the gas sails the energy they need, yes, I know. You've already told me it will allow the microchips to send back the information they gather on the atmosphere. I'm no scientist, but I can grasp the broad strokes."

Stan couldn't afford to talk down to the man. "I'm sorry. It's just that if we rush this and release more of the gas formula from the sails than is necessary, it could cause torrential downpours the likes of which the world has never seen."

"At this point that sounds like a blessing!" Banacheck spread his arms wide. "We're running out of food, Trotter. As it is right now, crops can't grow in the soil. There's no grass for our live-stock. We're running out of resources. You want to talk about something the likes of which the world has never seen? If we don't get rain soon, that's the kind of *famine* we'll be talking about."

Stan looked down at his clipboard, frowning at the latest cal-culations his team had come up with. Banacheck's smile was al-most too smug to bear. Stan noticed his tiepin, a diamond-en-crusted piece of gold opulence with a logo in the center, a trape-zium with a figure eight inside it. *Probably another gift from their mysterious silent partner*, Stan thought. He couldn't condemn their secret contributor, though. They could remain anonymous as long as they kept investing in the project.

Stan went to the window and stared out at the arid dirt of the field below where the laser satellites were lined up, a quarter of a mile between each. Beyond them was only a cracked wasteland of dead trees and dust.

"We're moving forward," Banacheck said. "The order has come down from the very top, Trotter. We'll be launching the mother-ship by the end of the week."

•••

Three red lights throbbed behind the haze like blurry suns. Seeing the shadowy outline of a building, a cry escaped Stan's lips and he smiled for the first time in days. Even though the safe haven may prove to be only temporary, it would be much safer than the boat, and they could wait there for the rescue barges to come once the storm died down. He wiped the rain from his eyes to see the mon-olith standing alone in this new sea, the other buildings having washed away or lying buried beneath. As if in an act of mercy, the waves calmed as their ship approached. The water was still choppy, but the boat was staying level.

"I can see a tower," he told Tara. "We should be able to dock there, sweetie."

Tara only whimpered in reply, but it was a welcome break from her screaming for her mommy. A siren wailed and a gruff voice came over the loudspeakers.

"Attempting to unload at the Hoover building," the voice informed them. "Do not attempt to exit the ship without the assistance of a crewman. Do not rush the loading platform. Parents with small children will be escorted first."

The skyscraper emerged out of the mist like a dead lighthouse. The crewmen pushed their way through the herd where grappling hooks were ready to fire and the anchor was ready to drop, though Stan doubted the anchor could even reach bottom now. As they reached the building he saw several abandoned boats latched onto the tower. Three of the building's windows at water level had been smashed out to serve as a loading dock, and Stan wondered how many other such docks were already underwater. The grappling hooks were fired. They connected with the tower, and as the lines pulled taut the ship swung and groaned, sending some of the passengers to the deck. A man went tumbling over the side and vanished into the black waters below. Stan held fast to the pole, and Tara to him.

The boat reached the edge of the skyscraper and they connected to the dock as best as they could. Instantly the mob pushed forward with no regard to parents carrying their children, and the crewmen were too outnumbered to hold back the stampede. Though he itched to leave the boat, Stan thought it was best for he and Tara to hold tight until the crowd thinned, and a moment later he was glad he'd stayed put. Too many people were charging the deck at once. Many began to slip. Stan watched in horror as the waves leapt up to devour them, their hands reaching helplessly as they were carried away into the sea of trash. But instead of this serving as a warning to the others, this only increased the mass hysteria. The crewmen clung to the bow as the frenzied crowd lunged, nearly as many failing to make it as those who did. Cries of panic rose over the storm in a hellish chorus. Stan had heard so many screams over the past few days. They would never stop echoing in his mind.

Once the crowd thinned, he came toward the edge of the ship and allowed the crewmen to do their job. They were helped across, and when it came time for Tara to be lifted to the edge she cried out for him, not wanting Stan to let her go.

"I'm coming right behind you," he told her.

"No! Stay with me!"

The crewman on the tower's dock looked at him with haunted, bloodshot eyes. Stan nodded and the man scooped Tara up as she

112

kicked and screamed. Stan crossed over as quickly as he could and took Tara in his arms again, thanking the man for prying her away.

"It's okay," he told her.

"Don't leave me, Daddy!"

Calling him *daddy* instead of *dad* made her seem all the more fragile, and put a deeper ache into his heart.

"No, never," he assured her. "No matter what happens, I'll always be with you."

Tara sniffled. "You mean, like angels?"

"Yeah, like angels. Now I've got to put you down, sweetie. My arms are tired."

She agreed only after he promised to hold her hand.

He had to get her dry. As they crossed the floor and moved around the rotting cubicles, Stan ran through it all in his head again, how the probes had been reprogrammed to emit excessive gas into the atmosphere, and how the gas formula his team had concocted had worked *too* well. It had been raining for nearly a month, having started only hours after the laser had carried the sails beyond the troposphere. The bastards on the council hadn't even had the patience to release a fraction of the formula and let the microchips gather information. They'd just released the gas and lots of it, thinking that more was better. This was the result of America's attack on intellectualism, Stan thought, of its anti-science leaders, of the *shoot first and ask questions later* philosophy. Ignorance and impatience had led to undoing.

Suddenly everyone's voices stopped at once and all Stan heard was the combined howl of the storm and the ominous creaking of the tower. The silence had come abruptly, like someone shutting off a television, and as he turned around Stan gasped and staggered backward. Where a good fifty people had been standing was now vacant. He and his daughter were alone.

"What in the—"

He stared in disbelief, too afraid to return to the edge of the dock. Had a massive wave come through the opening and sucked everyone into the water? Impossible. He would have seen and heard it. The ship was still there, but its passengers were gone. This floor of the building was open space but for the cubicles, and his back had only been turned to the crowd for a few seconds!

"Where did everybody go?" Tara asked.

It pained him to no longer have any answers. Fathers were

supposed to know.

"Hello?" he called, his voice echoing like a ghost.

"Daddy, I'm scared."

"I know, sweetie."

So am I, he thought.

He picked up his daughter, ignoring the soreness in his arms. She nuzzled into his neck and he savored the feel of her skin and the smell of her hair, unsure of how many more chances he'd get to enjoy them. But he got moving, not wanting to spend another minute on the same floor where the others had vanished into thin air. On the other end of the ceiling he saw a sign for the stairwell, ran to it and put Tara down. This time he was the one to insist they hold hands. There was a new fear in him now. If he didn't keep her close, could she disappear too?

After ascending to a higher floor, they exited the stairwell and came into a room that spanned the length of the building's east and north walls, giving them a panoramic view of the neon green lightning throbbing inside the nacreous clouds. Their speed was increasing exponentially, and the electricity in the air was unnatural, creating a strange iridescence. Looking at these lights, Stan wondered about the intense weather's potential for shifting the earth's magnetic field. Were the glow not so apocalyptic, it would be rather beautiful, an aurora borealis. But given the circumstances, the clouds seemed monstrous, like great membranes to a universe of utter destruction.

Don't play God. That's what Kate had always told him.

He saw a blanket draped across an office chair and half a roll of paper towels on a custodial cart—small gifts that meant so much to him he almost cried.

"It's a miracle!" Tara said with excitement.

He had her take off her top layers and soggy shoes, then dried her off with the towels and wrapped her in the blanket. He wrung out her sweater and jeans and placed them across the desk while she warmed up. He wouldn't let them sit there for long, though. She needed to be ready to move at a moment's notice.

But to where?

Unless one of the rescue barges came by, was there anywhere else to go?

He'd been hoping there would be other people in the tower with some information from the outside, even though it was impossible to get a phone signal. The electrical interference of the storms and all the collapsed cellular towers had seen to that. Everything was broken now, engulfed and dragged down into a liquid hell.

"Daddy, where is everybody?"

"I don't know. Stay close to me, okay?"

"Okay."

Pink was returning to her cheeks. Another small miracle. But still there was the anomaly of the other people vanishing. And what of the other boats tied to the building? Where were *those* people?

•••

After a rest, Tara redressed and they began exploring the tower. Starting with the floor they were on, they weaved in and out of halls and offices, finding no one. There were only desks and chairs and filing cabinets. But a few rooms had an unprofessional look to them, with candles and crystals spread about on windowsills. Stan wondered what Hoover Tower had been before all of this. An insurance building? A credit card company? He either couldn't remember or had never known, even though it was one of the tallest buildings in their small city. Though there was no power, he checked all the laptops in case one of them had a charge. Each had the same symbol on them, a corporate logo he paid little attention to. When he found a laptop that would start up, he wasn't surprised at the scrambled mess of the screen. The storms were wreaking havoc on all electronics. It was as if bolts of lightning had coursed through every one of them and fried their insides like a swarm of fire ants. When they came across a break room, Stan used a chair to smash the glass of a vending machine and gave Tara a Snickers. He had a brief but grim vision of them subsiding on candy and chips until they ran out and died of starvation.

No. He couldn't think like that. Help would come. Rescuers would come and—

And disappear, he thought. *Just like the others.*

What on earth had happened? They couldn't have just vaporized or been subsumed into space. And surely he wasn't hallucinating because Tara saw them vanish too.

"Let's try the next floor," he said.

They climbed to the top floor, the last stop. This one was wide open and completely empty. No cubicles or desks or chairs. No offices or hallways or restrooms. It looked incomplete, as if construction had stopped halfway. Steel girders and copper wire were visible in the walls and the floor was bare concrete, littered with papers and other debris.

Stan sighed. "Alright, sweetie, let's go back to that break room."

They turned toward the door to the stairwell.

It wasn't there.

Tara began to cry. "What's going on? I don't understand."

Stan ran to the blank wall where the door had been, running his hands over the smooth concrete in search of a hidden knob. He pounded at it with frustration. Its solidity was surreal, devastating. He cursed the wall, the tower, and the sheer madness of it all. Instead of answering his daughter, he repeated her.

"What's going on?"

The only explanations he could conceive of were preposterous—wormholes, a spacetime rip or abnormality had transported them to god knows where. It was either that or some sort of paranormal phenomena. Stan was a man of science, not science fiction, but it wasn't long ago that he never would have believed a storm would be big enough to do what this one had done, nor would he have believed in the intense lightning now ravaging electronics as well as the sky.

Realizing he had turned his back on Tara, he yelped in fear and spun around, relief warming him when he found her still there.

"Are we going to die, Daddy?"

His heart dropped. "No, sweetie, no, we're . . ."

Stan got down on one knee, hugged her tight and closed his eyes, and when he reopened them he looked out the window, seeing new colors and formations in the clouds. There was one massive cloud at the forefront in the shape of a mushroom, with long tendrils hanging out of it like ethereal veins. Pulsing fireworks glowed within it, making the cloud resemble a massive jellyfish. There were two similar clouds just behind it, drifting over the surface of the water as if sifting through the wreckage for prey. Stan and Tara went to the windows to get a closer look. These clumps of nimbus were so foreign looking that he wondered if they were clouds at all. They moved steadily, their flashes of light coming every few seconds, but always in unison. They almost seemed *alive*.

Stan gritted his teeth at what he may have created, or what he may have let through from . . . *somewhere else*.

The water level continued to rise.

Tara's right, you know. You are going to die here.

He led his daughter across the floor, searching for any kind of trapdoor or passageway to get to the floors below. His foot landed on a large sheet of paper he hadn't seen beneath the dust and he slipped and nearly lost his balance. Cursing, he kicked the paper away and it spun over, revealing the complex mathematical equations scribbled across it in black chalk. There were other papers just like this one, all scattered across the floor. Stan recognized calculus and topology, algebra and dynamical systems, all scrawled in a frenzied hand. He got down on one knee, pushing aside the melted blobs of candles, and skimmed through the papers. Most of them were in relation to physics. There were rambling, diary-like writings on strangelets and tachyons—hypothetical particles—and detailed records of the weather. The papers were all helter-skelter, many obviously missing from the complete text. But one of the papers had no basis in science, and this was the one that interested Stan the most, because on the paper was a symbol, the same as the corporate logos on all the laptops on the floors below, the same symbol revealed on the floor when he moved the papers away, the very one on Mr. Banacheck's tiepin.

It was a large trapezium, inside of which was a figure eight resembling a vertebra. Draped over the top was a half moon, lying on its side so the trapezium wore it like a hat. Bolts of lightning jutted out from all sides like the SS symbols the Nazis had used. He looked again at the candles lining the floor and shook his head at the absurdity he suggested to himself. Still, he read the sheet, his throat clicking dryly.

It started off in mid-sentence:

. . . a black mass for dark matter, a celebration of the opening of the veil between all worlds. Every possibility will be revealed. Every variation. Each new thunder crack is a door.

Here the symbol was drawn in the middle of the page.

The great storm tears our worlds apart to bring them closer together.

"What is it, Daddy?"

Stan blinked at the writing, which had left him cold. "I don't know."

"Was someone doing homework?" she asked, looking at the mess of numbers.

The silent partner, Stan thought. The mysterious, reclusive billionaire who had invested so much money in The Weather Plexors Project. Could this be his tower? Could he have lived up here, scribbling notes in his nightgown like a physics-obsessed Howard Hughes?

He returned to the papers, reading random snippets about the tearing of spacetime and the possibility for an infinite number of dimensions, of tachyon particles with the potential to move at the speed of light, and therefore through time. Interwoven with hard science statistics were quasi-religious prophesies about the apocalypse. Whoever had written the text seemed to believe the end of the world would actually incorporate the end of the spacetime continuum, that reality itself would be torn apart.

Stan's shoulders tensed when he thought of the vanishing people downstairs and the disappearing door, of the impossibility of the tsunamis and all that was happening. Could this be just the beginning? He remembered the eerie feeling he'd had all along that the Weather Plexors would disrupt more than the troposphere. Had it disturbed something cosmic, something humankind had never come to recognize or understand?

"Daddy . . ." Tara whispered.

Stan knew these thoughts of his were absurd, but logic was a hard thing to come by these days. Whoever had written these notes had a firm grasp on astrophysics. They understood something Stan didn't. It almost seemed as if the author had seen the storms as an opportunity.

Had this been the secret objective of Banacheck and his silent backer all along?

Stan scowled at the candles and the crude symbol chalked across the floor as if they were at an altar or in—

A church.

"Daddy," Tara repeated with more urgency.

He looked up, and before he could respond, his words froze in his throat. From their panoramic view of town, several different views began to overlap, each vista differing greatly. One moment, all Stan could see were decimated streets, the next, he could see the buildings below, perfectly intact, as if nothing had happened. There were lush spring days superimposed over blizzards of purple ice, the images shadowing each other as if they were drawn on tracing paper. With each flash there was an under image of the rising murk as it reached their floor. Tara shrieked as the windows wobbled from the pressure. Stan scooped her up again and started running, directionless, hoping for some sort of safety.

As the sea level rose to greet them, the random images entered the tower itself, and Stan became disoriented by people walking past him one moment and then vanishing the next. Some of them were the survivors from the fishing boat, scrambling for higher ground. Others were construction workers putting walls up, and others were office workers having a busy day on the fully finished floor, each of them bestowed with the emblem. Every person represented a different variation of the place Stan was standing, an alternate reality. And outside the windows, the ominous cloud entities encircled the tower, their nebulous forms pulsating with colors he had never seen.

In a flash, a longhaired man in a raincoat and rubber hat appeared. He was sitting on the floor in the middle of the symbol, surrounded by candles as he scribbled in a notebook. Stan's own reports on the Weather Plexors were spread out in fans.

The investor.

The door for the stairwell reappeared, and Stan bolted toward it with Tara clutching him tight. The water had risen up the shaft like an overflowing well, its level already washing over Stan's shins. Pounding thunder made a demon's song with his daughter's screams, and Stan ran up the stairs with the water chasing his heels, a tornado of black sludge rising up the concrete throat of the tower. He tried not to think of the stairwell vanishing while they were still in it. Would the concrete that replaced it crush them, or would they vanish with it, into some other time, some other place? He reached the final door and pressed against the lever, then tucked his body around Tara, shielding her as they emerged onto the roof and into the cold, dark heart of the hurricane.

The world was many.

As the different dimensions and timelines converged, stars appeared and lightning cracked. Buildings rose and crumbled. Multiple suns—each at different spots in the sky—glowed and bled. Birds and insects and creatures Stan could not identify sailed in and out of time, blipping like static through the air. He saw daylight and darkness simultaneously. There was a living world beneath one flooded and uprooted. Every possible version of the world he had called home converged into one frenetic amalgam, a new reality made of multiple ones. He no longer knew where he existed. Even when he shut his eyes he could hear the sounds of the different realities, some alive and colorful, some hollow with death. The only thing grounding him was his sense of touch. He could feel the rain of his true world pounding down upon him. Though the dimensions were overlapping, he was still grounded in his own.

A soft wave flowed across the back of his legs. The tower was being consumed.

Through the hyperrealism, Stan spotted the square shape of the storage unit, a concrete shed that was part of the structure itself. He stumbled toward it.

"Hold on to my shoulders," he told Tara, positioning her for a piggyback ride.

There was a steel ladder attached to the shed. He climbed it to the top where the power converters were. Looking past the layers of worlds, he could still see the underlined imprint of his own, a world that was nothing but a murderous ocean.

He and Tara hugged each other in a silent farewell.

The yellow daylight of one of the overlapping worlds fluttered like a strobe light, and then there was a sound Stan recognized— a steady, mechanical thrum. He looked up, past the murk of his world and into the one lined up almost perfectly over it, making it the clearest of the other dimensions. Black bars spun like the blades of a ceiling fan across a clear blue sky.

It came into view like a mirage, the shape of a hovering rescue chopper with people inside looking down at them. Though the storm of his world raged around him, Stan could feel this new world's sunshine on his cheeks. Glancing over the ledge of the building, he saw the super-imposed image of this new, sunny world. It was in tatters, probably from the aftermath of storms. It seemed this timeline had suffered the tsunamis and rain, but not to the degree his own world had. This world was still habitable.

"Daddy! Look!"

In his own world, the ocean of filth surged around his waist. He stood at his full height on top of the highest part of the shed, placing Tara on his shoulders and into the light of the other dimension.

"Reach!" he told her.

He could smell the dry air the helicopter blew across his face, even as the storm raged below him. They were at the threshold now—existing in two dimensions at once, twin worlds with a difference of life and death. Another wave hit him. He could taste the salt water, but Tara was standing on his shoulders. A police-woman dangled from a harness, reaching for his daughter from across space and time. Tara's feet left Stan just as the wave slammed into him, and he held on to a power converter to stay in place just long enough to say goodbye.

"Daddy!" Tara cried. "Don't leave me!"

The world of sunshine was growing fainter, the overlap going off center as the clouds passed. But Tara was safe now, safe in a better reality. The chopper hovered, a faded wraith. A rope ladder was thrown and his hands went right through the material when he touched it, as if it were made of smoke.

"Don't leave me, Daddy!"

"Never!" he called out to her. "I'm always with you! Like an angel!"

The sunlight was enveloped by the storms, and he heard his daughter yelling for him, but the sound of her voice had become a metallic echo, like playing telephone with tin cans and a line of string. The amorphous cloud entities howled with thunder, their hazy bodies flickering as they retreated from the temple of Hoover Tower. The rain came down, Stan's world returning to him in its horrible entirety, but even as the freezing ocean engulfed him, he couldn't help but smile at his one final miracle.

JAILBAIT FRANKENSTEIN

I'M NOT A PEDOPHILE. LET'S make that clear right now.

Never have I sexually assaulted or molested a *child*, nor have I even fantasized of doing such a thing. After all, I'm not a pervert or a monster. I'm merely a man—a man with his own tastes, just like anybody else. Can I help it if I am attracted to teenagers? Just because I'm forty-seven doesn't mean I have to like forty-seven-year-old women, does it? I would hope not, because I simply cannot do it. No matter how physically attractive a woman my own age might be, they could never spark my interest the way teenage girls do.

It's not necessarily their bodies, or even their youth itself that makes them more alluring. It's their playful, carefree nature—their innocence. This light radiates off them. They're seeing the world for the first time and therefore have not been beaten down by it. They have none of the cynicism of adult women, none of the cruel sarcasm or nihilistic viewpoints on life itself. Their dreams are fresh instead of shattered and discarded. They look at men with curiosity instead of distrust, having not had their hearts broken yet. Their laughter is warm and pure, not sardonic and jabbing. Girls still have the potential to be and feel and love anything, whereas women are so far removed from their own free will they are a living, breathing rut.

I say this not out of sexism. I look at boys and men in this exact same regard. Boys are bright and clean; men are brutal and filthy, and far worse than women could ever deign to be. But my romantic leanings are heterosexual, so the innocence of boys, while pure, is of little interest to me.

Maybe I long for a teenage girl because of some yearning to "go home again," an atypical reaction to my aging. Facing one's mortality makes you long for your lost youth and fills you with regrets, leaving you haunted by what might have been. But I doubt this mid-life crisis theory really applies to me, as I have *always* preferred teenage girls, from the instant of my sexual awakening to this very moment, here in this dank basement. And what brought me here was a yearning for at least one more of them, a budding girl-child I could embrace, for only they hold the key that unlocks the prison of my anhedonia, this emotional deficiency that makes it impossible for me to derive pleasure from all the things others find enjoyable.

•••

I first saw her from the back.

She was petite, and yet she had a round apple of a bottom, full and high and luscious in her summer jean-shorts. Tanned legs gave way to two tiny feet that would make a foot fetishist foam, placed inside open toe shoes with tall heels, accentuating her perfect ass. She wore a pale blue spaghetti-strap top and her platinum blonde hair was long and flat until the bottom, where it curled into coils that bounced as she walked down the sidewalk in front of the high school.

My breath stopped in my throat and my hands tightened on the steering wheel. I rode the brake, giving me more time to admire her on my way to work. I always took this route so I could view all the girls as they carried their books and played with their phones as they made their way to class. No, I wasn't stalking any one of them in particular, and I *never* called out to them or tried to lure them to my car. As I've already said, I'm not a pedophile. *Looking* is hardly a crime. Besides, who's to say where the line is really crossed? How is the totally legal eighteen-year-old birthday girl of today any different from the illegal seventeen-year-old she was yesterday? It wasn't like these girls aren't sexually active anyway. This was a high school, not a playground. I shouldn't have to apologize just for looking.

As I drove past this fine specimen, I turned my head as far as it would go, shameless in my rubbernecking, and I was rewarded for it with two of the biggest breasts I had ever seen on a girl her age. Obviously they were the first thing to catch my eye, and they held my gaze for as long as I could see her. Full, round and tight to her chest, they winked out of the low top covering nothing higher than her nipples. My mouth went dry, and I was only snapped out of those boobs' hypnotic spell when a car horn blared. I swerved back into my lane and narrowly missed a head-on collision. Straightening in my seat, I had just enough time to look at my little Lolita in the rearview mirror and catch a glimpse of her horrible, horrible face.

•••

I was useless all day at work, sitting at my desk, looking into the computer but not registering the information, seeing only the nightmare of that face. It had been so alien. The eyes were slanted, giving them a feline appearance. Her lips were swollen—not what you'd call bee-stung, but truly swollen, as if infected. Her nose was too small for her face and its tip pointed upward toward long, thin eyebrows that looked as if they'd been tattooed on. When I'd seen that face, I nearly collided with yet another car. While human, the face was bizarrely warped, as if I was seeing it in a funhouse mirror instead of my rearview one.

She must be deformed, I thought.

Having seen her face from a distance (and through a mirror), I wasn't exactly sure what was wrong with her. Perhaps she had been in an accident. With a body like hers, it was hard to believe she had some sort of genetic issue. I felt almost certain she had not always looked that way. Something had changed her.

I told my boss I wasn't feeling well so I could go home a little early. What I really wanted was to be able to drive by the high school when it was letting out, so I might see the deformed girl again. The stark contrast of her amazing body and grotesque face had possessed me. I had to get a better look.

Arriving at the school just before it normally let out, I parked in the front lot, which led out to the sidewalk where I had seen the girl that morning. I couldn't be sure she would take the same route, but figured this was my best shot. As I sat there waiting, I wondered what her life must be like. Clearly it was normal enough if she went to school, but she must be a social outcast. I'd always been socially awkward, a loner, but I couldn't imagine the kind of blackballing this poor girl must have endured. Despite her delectable body, her face was a curse. She was what people called a "butterface," as in "she has a hot body, all *but her face.*" For this I sort of pitied her; though I have never been able to feel empathy, I could still comprehend it. But above pity I felt curiosity, and despite her ghastliness I wondered what her sex life might be like, if indeed she had one. Was there someone in her class who wasn't at all picky—someone who couldn't *afford* to be picky? Some guys will overlook an ugly face for the sake of a beautiful body, and teenage hormones make a growing boy do crazy things. And was I much different? Here I was, just sitting in my car and waiting to get another look at this girl. Was it really just morbid curiosity now that I was thinking about her sex life?

When the clock struck the hour the doors to the school swung open, unleashing a throng of students into the parking lot. Some climbed aboard buses and piled into cars while others went to the bike rack or started home on foot. I scanned the crowd for my girl and tried not to get too distracted by looking at other ones. The voices of youth were like a melody and they took me to a faraway world, a memory of something that may not have existed. As the teens walked past and around my car, the soft flesh of their nubile forms gleamed in the sunlight, and I found this very telling, the perfect symbolism for the light they exuded. Their beauty delighted and devastated me at the same time. I could not help but smile up at them, but not a single girl so much as glanced in my direction. To these fluttering little angels, I was invisible.

When the initial rush passed, a second wave of teenagers came down the front steps and spilled into the early summer air, giddy they only had another week until the school year ended. This bunch also ignored me, and who could blame them? I was a graying husk of a man with pockmarks and a paunch. There was no room for people like me in their universe. They walked around my car as if it was empty, and seeing their carefree happiness made me feel ruined beyond repair.

The crowd thinned until there was but a single girl standing in front of my car, a girl who looked directly at me with cat-like eyes.

It's her.

I sat up straight, sweat forming at my temples and in my armpits, and loosened the tie that now seemed to be strangling me. I had not seen her come out of the school. It was as if she had appeared out of nothing. The girl was in front of my car but was a good fifteen feet away and the sunlight was harsh. I still couldn't get a close look at her. I would have to wait for her to walk past.

But she wasn't moving.

She just stood there like a mannequin as other students moved around her, and all the time she looked directly at me, causing me to tingle with a nervousness that made my whole body feel as if it had fallen asleep. I began to argue with myself.

Should I get out of the car?

No, you idiot! What are you going to do, approach a young girl on school grounds? That's a good way to get the cops called. Besides, what on earth would you say to her?

Maybe I can just walk past her as if I have business inside the school, that way I can get a good look at her.

No, stay in the car! Stay in the car!

But I didn't.

The rational voice in my head lost the argument and I stepped out into the cruel light of day and closed the car door behind me. I tried not to look directly at the girl, hoping it would seem like I was walking toward the school instead of her. Still she did not budge. I began to sweat, my legs turning to jelly. When I snuck glances at her, she was always looking directly at me, her eyes flashing behind the taut meat of her face, the fat earthworms of her lips quivering beneath a thick coat of glossy red lipstick. The closer I drew, the more pronounced her breasts appeared—huge and perfect, nipples standing at attention beneath the top. I gulped, and when I got close enough I dared to look her face to face, planning to do so just long enough to satisfy my strange desire. After all, she must have been used to people staring at her. She was a sideshow freak, a sexualized Joseph Merrick, like something out of a late-night B-movie. My chest tightened as if my heart had stopped. I couldn't blink and my legs stopped moving on their own accord.

My god . . .

The girl's face was not just deformed; it was *altered*. Up close, I could see the changes to her face had been deliberate. The skin was pulled tight and pinched at her neck and hairline, airbrushed and spray-tanned. The slant of her eyes was forced, as if someone had tried to make her look Asian but had overstated the effect, giving her an animalistic appearance, and the eyes themselves wore contacts that turned them an unnatural, sparkling purple. Her lips were not bruised; they were purposely inflated. She was a raging brew of collagen and botox, a puzzle of nips and tucks, plastic surgery gone berserk.

She looked up at me with a bleached smile.

"Hello, handsome."

•••

"What?"

"I called you handsome," she said with a giggle. She went up on her tippy toes and then back down onto her heels, then repeated the motion. She held her books over her crotch and as she bobbed her huge breasts jiggled. "Hasn't anyone ever called you handsome before?"

Words tumbled down my brain but failed to reorganize in my mouth.

"Well . . . ah . . . I, um . . ."

She giggled again in the way only teenage girls do.

"I saw you this morning," she said. "You know, *looking* at me."

My jaw tightened. "I . . . I was just . . ."

"Hey, it's okay. I like to be admired by men. I consider it a compliment. Especially when they're *real* men, *grown* men."

When she spoke, her lips pursed and her huge eyelashes throbbed. She tried to make expressions, but her flesh was too hard and taut. It was like someone talking beneath a snug Halloween mask.

She twirled her hair in one finger. "You do like what you see, don't you?"

I looked around the schoolyard, terrified that someone might have overheard.

"Let's go to your car," she said.

"What?"

"You heard me. Come on, it's okay, just calm down. You can give me a ride home."

She started walking but I was glued to where I stood. Everything whirled around me in a blur and I had to take deep breaths to keep from fainting. The girl opened the passenger side door.

This was really happening.

•••

"My name's Barbie."

I wiped at my brow to keep the sweat out of my eyes and turned left down Main Street, as she had directed.

"Really? *Barbie?*"

"Yeah. What's yours?"

"Phil," I lied. I didn't want to give her any information. This

127

could be considered abduction. Besides, I wasn't sure what was really going on. "My name is Phil."

"Well, Phil. You still haven't answered my question."

"What question?"

"Do you like what you see?"

The hairs on my arms rose as she cupped her breasts in her hands and squeezed. She licked her lips, running the silver tongue-bar across them.

I blinked in disbelief. "What . . . what're you doing?"

She giggled and put her hand on my thigh. I quivered.

"Sorry," she said, "I'm, like, so bad at this!"

Her playfulness filled me with butterflies. Beneath all of that knotted flesh, she was still a girl, still young and inexperienced. And that's what really did it for me—the *innocence*. That's what could rekindle my long-extinguished fire. Looks were a bonus, but not a necessity. If the girl still retained her youthful exuberance and had not yet been tainted by the cruelty of being alive, then she was a jewel plucked from the treasure I'd been hunting all of my adult life.

"You can probably tell," she said.

"Tell what?"

She blushed. "That I'm a virgin."

Barbie smiled wide when she said this, and I admired her braces with their pink rubber bands. She seemed younger with each passing moment, and my hands moistened on the wheel, my tongue darting out to wet my parched lips.

Now her face didn't bother me as much as it had when I'd first seen it.

She squeezed my thigh and my loins stirred.

"I'm just sort of, like, drawn to older men," she said. "Boys my age just don't understand me. They don't appreciate everything I'm doing to be beautiful."

"Oh? What is it that you're doing?"

"All these improvements," she said, running her hands across her face. "All of these surgeries to make me perfect. Some people think I had to have them done, that I was in an accident. But no. I'm becoming beautiful for the sake of beauty. People think I'm too young for these improvements, but Daddy knows what he's doing."

I cocked an eyebrow. "Your father did them?"

"Yeah, he's a brilliant plastic surgeon and dedicated to making me perfect. He's giving me the perfect body—a new butt, new boobs, new face. He wants me to be the most beautiful girl in the world. That's why he named me Barbie."

I wondered if it was legal for the man to do this, and what the girl's mother might think. I decided not to ask. We drove through a wooded neighborhood, Barbie giving me directions along the way. As we continued on, the houses grew farther apart, and low, somber clouds drifted across the sun, muting it.

"You really walk this far?" I asked.

Barbie didn't answer; she just told me to take the next right. She took her phone from her pocket and sent a quick text, then put it away again without making mention of it. The road was crumbling and grass grew up through the cracks like corn stalks. There were no houses or driveways here, only a long row of woods on either side. The storms of summer afternoons were steadily approaching now, turning the sky to onyx and dulling the colors of the trees. It began to drizzle. The road curved and as we went around the bend a two-story house came into view. It was as ashen as the day had become, with a roof that seemed out of proportion with the rest of the structure. The windowsills were crumbling with wood rot and part of the gutter hung loose. There were no cars in the cracked and oil-stained driveway, and the lawn was a dead brown hellscape. Was this really the house of a surgeon? As we drew closer, the drizzle turned to full-on rain.

"This is it?" I asked, trying to hide my disappointment that the ride was over.

"Yeah."

When I pulled alongside the front of the house, there was a sudden pop and hiss, and the whole car fell forward and shuddered.

"Damn it!"

Barbie gasped. "What was that?"

"It's the tires."

I stopped the car and got out, the rain pelting me so hard I had to shield my eyes with my hand. The front driver's side tire was completely flat. I walked to the passenger side. The other tire had the same damage.

"Damn it!" I said again, having only one spare.

I knelt to assess the damage. Given that the tires deflated immediately, I doubted Fix-A-Flat would be much help. When I got down low, I saw the huge roofing nails littering the roadside. I clenched my fists and was soaked by the time I got back in the car.

"Is everything okay?" Barbie asked.

"No. The tires have blown out. Someone threw big nails in the road!"

"Oh no." A look of childish hurt fell upon Barbie, one so strong it was visible despite the concrete of her face. She picked at her fingernails and hung her head, cuter than a lost puppy. "I'm sorry, Phil. If you hadn't given me a ride . . ."

"No, no. This isn't your fault. I guess I'll have to call a tow truck."

I took my phone from my pocket and Barbie reached for my hand.

"Don't bother," she said. "There's no service out here."

I glanced at the screen and saw she was right. No bars. I sighed.

"We have a landline," she said. "Why don't you come inside?"

Her hand went back to my thigh, caressing. I so wanted to join her, but . . .

"I really shouldn't," I said.

"Come on. Nobody's home. My dad is out of town, at a medical conference. It'll be just you and me."

Her hand slid farther up my thigh, getting closer to the Promised Land. I admit my desire got the better of me in that moment and obliterated what little good sense I had.

•••

It was dark inside the house, the only light being that of the gray day seeping through the cracked blinds. I could make out the shapes of furniture and the black holes of the doors lining the hallway. Barbie held my hand, guiding me through the dimness.

"Want to see my room?" she asked.

My heart raged inside my chest, my every pore offering sweat.

"I suppose," I said.

She led me down the hallway to the last door and turned the loose knob. A cold draft rose up from where a set of concrete stairs descended into darkness.

"My room's in the basement," she said.

"Oh."

"I like it." The lavender of her eyes twinkled with adolescence. "It's like my own little apartment."

Something about the thickness of the blackness below gave me a moment of hesitation, and Barbie sensed my tension when she tried to guide me. She turned to me, ran her hand through my thinning hair, and gave me a soft kiss on the cheek. The smell and feel of the girl electrified me. I quivered with delight before following her, and halfway down the stairs she turned on a light, bringing into focus a scene of horror so intense I froze when I should have run. Beside me, Barbie giggled.

Two stainless steel tables were side by side in the center of the room, bolted to the concrete floor. Several wheeled carts and smaller tables surrounded them, each carrying various scalpels and other surgical tools, some of which were speckled with blood. On one wall was a metal shelving unit, filled with jars containing random pieces of flesh and human remains soaking in pale green fluid.

Two men were suspended from the ceiling by chains that bound their wrists, both naked, both missing huge portions of their skin. Perfect squares of flesh had been cut away from their bodies, leaving glistening, crimson wounds, and one of the men had a gorge carved around his midsection where the fat of his love handles had been removed. Their faces were bloody pulp, void of skin and features, the lips and noses missing, bulging eyes staring at me. The men moaned, still alive.

I opened my mouth to scream but something slammed against my spine and I fell hard, my knees cracking on the concrete. I turned my head and saw a man in hospital scrubs and a blood-slicked apron. He swung the crowbar once more, sending me into oblivion.

•••

I may have lost minutes or hours. I couldn't be sure how much time had passed once I awoke. However long it was, it had been enough time for them to strip and suspend me from another set of chains. My head and back were fused in a tight ball of pain that ran the length of me, and my mind was in a fog, half delirious from a possible concussion, in denial of my reality and trying to convince myself this was a nightmare.

I heard Barbie's voice. "He's waking up, Daddy."

My eyes came into focus as Barbie's father approached me. He was a slender man with hard eyes and slicked back hair. A surgeon's mask hung below his chin.

"Hello, Todd."

He knew my real name. He must have gone through my wallet. "Please . . . let me go . . ."

"Let's skip this part," he said. "Spare me the begging and the telling me that you won't say anything to anyone. And don't bother telling me you have money or anything else you can give me in exchange for your freedom. You're here now, and that's that."

My body trembled, shoulders threatening to pop from the strain of being suspended from the rafters.

"What do you want?" I asked.

"Your skin." He said this frankly, sniffed. "That should be obvious enough, right?"

He patted my cheek with a hand sheathed by a latex glove.

I flinched. "My . . . *skin*?"

"Yes."

I looked at the other men hanging from the ceiling, their peeled torsos making promises of suffering to come.

Tears came to my eyes. "What do you want with my skin?"

The doctor slipped his arm around his daughter's shoulders. Barbie leaned her head against him, daddy's little girl.

"My baby girl needs it," the doctor said. "Skin grafts have to come from somewhere. Usually the patient will have some of their own skin removed and placed upon the area that needs it, but why should my daughter have to make such sacrifices?"

"She doesn't need skin!"

"Of course she does. Does she look complete to you?"

I looked toward the smiling girl. "Complete?"

"She's a work in progress. Art takes time, draft after draft until it reaches perfection."

"I'm going to be perfect," Barbie added.

"That's right, baby," he said, then turned back to me. "But we need skin, body fat, and connective tissue. We need fat to plump certain areas, like the lips, and skin to make alterations to the most important part—her face. She's young now, but we need to retain that youth, to perfect it. We must freeze her good looks in time with plastic, grafts, and expert modifications. Your skin may be older, Todd, but there are still parts of every man that are smooth and soft, and the flesh is malleable in the hands of a doctor dedicated to his craft. Barbie must have eternal youth if we're going to keep catching men like you."

I swallowed hard. "What do you mean by that?"

"Perverts," he said. "Pederasts and diddlers who like little girls."

"No, no. You don't understand—"

"Save it! Every one of you pedophiles have an excuse for why you are the filth that you are. I don't want to hear yours."

"But I've never done anything to anyone! I was just giving her a ride home."

"You were stalking me," Barbie said.

"No! I always drive past that school."

"Ha ha! I don't even go to that school. I'm home schooled."

The doctor nodded. "Society wouldn't understand why I operate on my daughter. They'd try to take her away from me."

"Then why was she there?"

"I go by places where other teens are," Barbie said. "Because that's where perverts go. I was bait."

"*Bait?*"

The doctor scowled. "And you took it. You were following my fifteen-year-old daughter down into a basement. Don't try to tell me your intentions were innocent."

Again Barbie giggled her girlish laugh and squeezed her breasts just as she had in the car, mocking me. I hoped I could convince the man I had meant no harm, but before I could come up with anything there was a movement in the shadows behind them, and when the figure came into the light I cried out and recoiled in my restraints.

"We know exactly what you were going to do," this monster said in a wet, feminine voice.

Huge clown lips dribbled saliva as she spoke, making her sound like she was blubbering. Her face was massive, taking up almost half her head as her ears stretched to the back of her skull. Her skin was dimpled and various shades, a jigsaw of races, and her eyes were wide, eyelids non-existent, giving her an appearance of frozen shock. She wore a tight cocktail dress, revealing the impossible hourglass of her figure, a body crippled by implants and corsets, morphed into a macabre cartoon of a pin-up girl.

"Hi, Mom," Barbie said. "How'd I do?"

"Wonderful as always," the mom-thing said. "You've bagged another one."

I looked at the other men, then back at Barbie. She winked at me.

"Look, I'm sorry," I said. "I never meant any harm."

The woman glared at me. "No harm?"

"No, none."

133

She stepped over to me, her swollen head casting a long shadow across my face.

"You think having *sex* with *children* causes no harm?"

"I didn't . . . didn't mean . . ."

"Barbie isn't our first child, but she's our *only* child. You see, there was another man, quite like you, Todd, who also thought having sex with children was harmless—at least, harmless for him. He raped children all the time and had no qualms about it, other than not wanting to get caught. So when he finished fucking them, he strangled them to death and buried their bodies under his porch, just like he did when he kidnapped our little Darla."

I couldn't breathe. Sweat boiled across my nude body as my stomach turned over.

"The police got to him before we could," she said. "We may not be able to get the revenge we wanted on him, but we can certainly take it out on the rest of you scum." The woman brushed her hair off of her shoulders like a grotesque movie star. "In the process, we might as well harvest what we need to stay beautiful."

The whole family glared at me like a pack of predators, and the doctor handed his daughter a gleaming scalpel.

"Show our guest what the rest of his short life will be like," he said.

Barbie moved toward me, and for the first time since I'd met her she was no longer girlish. She was as hard as granite, her warped face returning to the abomination I'd initially perceived it to be. There was no light to this teenage girl, no carefree youthfulness. Those traits were mere illusions, tools she'd honed to lure in her prey, knowing our weaknesses. I know now the innocence I'd searched for in her had been erased long ago, leaving her with a heart as broken and twisted as her face, and a void that could only be filled by men like me.

WE ALL SCREAM

LILY SHIVERED AT THE SOUND of "Turkey in the Straw."

She turned toward the noise—a horrible, metallic music that echoed off the houses of her neighborhood.

She didn't see the truck yet. There was still time.

Putting her Barbie dolls into the basket at the front of her bike, she climbed aboard and put her sneakers into the grips of the peddles. Shaking now, she had trouble keeping her balance and wished Mom hadn't made her take the training wheels off, but she was almost six and a half and the others kids had started making fun of her. Home wasn't far away—she *always* stuck to the block—but she sure wasn't going to walk the bike. Panic had seized her. It was the same kind of panic she'd felt on Halloween when a man with a chainsaw had chased her. She knew now the chain was off, making the saw harmless, and he was just playing his part at the haunted house (he stopped the saw and took off his scary mask when she'd begun to cry), but at the time panic had ripped through her like the talons of a vulture.

That had been a simple Halloween prank, but there was *nothing* funny about the ice cream truck, nothing at all. It was deathly serious. All the kids in Crestwood knew that. Her teacher, Mrs. Claiborne, had even done a special presentation about it, and they'd practiced drills in the school parking lot, using the short school bus as a stand-in for the truck.

Regaining her balance, Lily stood as she peddled to go as fast as possible, the warm air of early summer fluttering her blonde hair and the ribbons of her handlebars. She heard parents yelling from their porches and saw the other kids scrambling to get inside their houses. Garage doors came down and an old man walking his dog began to jog, even though it was clearly a strain for him to do so.

The repetitive melody grew louder, closer.

You're okay, Lily told herself. *You're okay.*

She rounded the corner to Emerson Road, afraid she might meet the truck head-on even though the sound was coming from behind her.

Don't look back.

But as she rounded the corner, the street behind her came into her side view, and out of the corner of her eye she saw the big white truck creeping along the road like the head of a funeral procession. Lily's teeth chattered, palms clammy on the handlebars. She struggled to hold in tears. The sign for Harper Lee Dr. was just ahead—her street—and she promised God she would never play down the block again, even if it was where the woods gave access to the small creek where she liked to play, letting her Barbies swim with Ken and get suntans.

As she turned onto her street, she saw plump Mrs. Weinberg in her front yard. She held a shotgun in her hands. In the window behind her the heads of her two boys peeked through the curtains. When she saw Lily, her eyes went wide and she pointed toward Lily's house.

"Get home, Lily!" the plump woman ordered her. "Get your butt inside *right now!*"

Lily didn't respond. There was no time to. The sound of the truck was drawing closer. Had it followed her? Had it *chosen* her? She whispered a prayer and wished, not for the first time, that her daddy still lived at home with them. She skidded into the front lawn and threw down her bike instead of standing it up properly like she was supposed to. That didn't matter right now. There was no car in their driveway, and Lily whimpered at the absence of Mom.

"Tommy!" she cried.

Whenever Aunt Rita couldn't watch them, her twelve-year-old brother was in charge during the hour or so between when they got home from school and when Mom came home after one of her mid-day shifts. While this injustice usually infuriated Lily, she now ached for her brother's protection, and when he opened the front door she nearly leapt into his arms.

"Ew," he grunted. "Why are you hugging me, twerp?"

"The truck is coming!" she said, tears spilling.

Tommy's face tightened, the freckles on the bridge of his nose swarming like fire ants. Always antagonistic, he shook his head in disgust and crossed his pudgy arms.

"There ain't no stupid truck, Lily."

"Just listen!" she shouted, pulling him out of the door jamb.

The haunting melody chimed louder than ever.

"Yeah, yeah," Tommy said. "I know there's *an* ice cream truck, but it's not the one everybody says it is."

Lily couldn't believe how he was acting. He was often incredulous and sardonic, laughing at her for putting a newly expunged tooth under her pillow and for never walking under ladders, but this was different. He needed to take this seriously.

"What are you talking about?" she said. "This is for real, Tommy!"

He made a *pfft* sound and turned back inside. Lily followed, flipping the locks on the door as Tommy hopped over the sofa and returned to his video game.

"We have to call Mom!" Lily said.

"No way. She's at work. You know we can only call her for emergencies."

"But this *is* an emergency!"

"No it isn't! God, you're such a baby. As long as you stay in your house, everything's supposed to be fine, right? Not that it matters, anyway. This is all bull crap."

Lily pulled back the curtain, watching and waiting, her little heart ricocheting off her ribs.

"It's not bull crap! If it was bull crap nobody would be scared."

Tommy paused his game, the warriors frozen in mid-dismemberment.

"Twerp, don't you get it? It's just another one of those stories adults tell kids to keep them in line. Just like the elf on the shelf."

"But the truck is right outside! It's coming!"

He shook his head and his smugness made Lily's fists clench. She wanted to hit him sometimes.

"They probably pay somebody to come through in a truck every summer," he said. "We're almost outta school for summer vacation, so they're giving us an early warning. Don't you get it? They scare us into staying close to our houses so we don't wander off and get into trouble."

Lily stomped her foot. "I don't believe you! I just saw Mrs. Weinberg. She had a gun, Tommy! A big gun!"

He made his dubious *pfft* sound again. "That's 'cause she's a Mom too. It's all an act and they're all in on it."

Lily steamed as she turned back to the window. Their tabby cat, Bibbo, jumped onto the sill and rubbed into her arm. Lily didn't want to believe a word Tommy was saying, but he'd been right about the Easter Bunny and the Boogeyman, and she was old enough to know that adults lied, at least sometimes. Any child of divorce knew that. But she'd been raised to fear Crestwood's ice cream truck, and fear was a hard thing to let go of, much harder than the magic of gift-giving rabbits. And she *definitely* still believed in Santa and his reindeer, no matter what Tommy said. Santa was real. She *knew* he was. Believing in him was just like believing in God. You didn't have to *see* him to know he existed. This rule also applied to whatever was inside that horrible truck. It was there whether you'd seen it or not, whether you believed in it or not.

Lily pressed her face to the glass to get a better view down the street, wanting to see the truck and yet not wanting to see it. She needed to know where it was, but was afraid to look at it head on, knowing she wasn't supposed to. Her brother stewed behind her.

"What?" Tommy asked. "You don't believe me?"

She shook her head. "Nu-uh!"

He snorted a laugh. "Fine. I'll prove it to you."

•••

His sister was screaming at him.

Tommy chuckled, his adolescent bravado leading him down the front steps. As much as Lily cried, she wouldn't leave the doorway, and she held the door half closed, keeping it over her like a shield. She was a little chicken twerp, but Tommy was twelve now. He knew the score and wasn't afraid to show it. In fact, he liked the idea of proving himself right. He strutted down the driveway, chin high, defiant even as he saw the truck round the corner.

It came at a turtle's pace, more idling than driving, a tall truck old-fashioned in design. Though it was painted white, there were dark blotches of dirt and other stains encrusted over it. The tires were bald and one of the headlights was missing, tufts of black exhaust farting out the back like dragon's breath, subsuming the truck in a fog. At first, Tommy shivered at the sound of it back-firing, but then he laughed it off.

They're really playing this up, he thought.

Tommy wondered who was driving it. There were large dash-board windows but they were tinted so darkly he couldn't see in-side. It was all part of the act as far as Tommy was concerned; after all, according to the legend, nobody was ever behind the wheel of the truck. That was part of its spookiness.

Maybe all the adults in the neighborhood take turns. Maybe Mom's not even at work right now, huh? Maybe she's trying to give us a good scare, to make sure we stay close to the house now that she's working afternoons. Well, good luck, driver, whoever you are. Tommy Dunne ain't buying it, no way.

Like everyone else, he'd been afraid of the truck as a child. But as he'd learned the truth about so many fairy tales and holiday traditions, he'd become a skeptic, and a cynical one at that. He told himself he was old enough to know this was all a scam, but at the base of his spine there was still a tremor, and he responded to it by pushing himself forward, denying his fear, wanting to prove to himself he didn't really feel it.

Tommy thought it was insulting how far the adults pushed this. A few years ago, the mayor had even put a ban on all ice cream trucks, even though this one was clearly different from all the others. It was so much bigger and dingier, a shuddering hull of a vehicle. Of course, Crestwood was the only town this ban ap-plied to because it was the only one that subscribed to such a ri-diculous myth. No other place had an evil *ice cream truck*. But then again, no other town had the strange stories that were said to have started with the truck and the items it sold, none of which were said to be ice cream.

Time to find out.

Tommy crossed to the sidewalk, watching the hulking truck as it approached. He looked to the Weinberg house, but Mrs. Weinberg was no longer in her yard. She too had ducked inside with her shotgun, playing her role to a T. He could see Bobby and Jayden Weinberg's faces in the window, each of them pale as chalk as they watched him with giant eyes. It put an extra swagger in Tommy's step to know every kid in the neighborhood would be watching, and he looked to Harmony Sagal's house, hoping his crush was seeing how bold he was, but the glare of the sun kept him from seeing into the windows. It didn't matter. The few people who weren't watching would hear about this, and afterward he'd be known as the bravest kid on the block and would bask in his newfound popularity.

Still, a cold sweat formed at the small of his back. He heard his sister calling for him, but she sounded so faint, as if she was across the other side of a lake instead of just four houses down from where he stood. He was only a few feet away from the truck when it stopped, letting him approach on his own. The exhaust smog rose all around it and Tommy was surprised by its odor. It didn't smell like oil and gas; it smelled like something sweet, like freshly baked cookies or hot oatmeal. Up close now, he saw the blotches weren't just stains, but also huge patches of rust, scratches and dents, as if the truck had long been under attack. Some of the marks were streaked with what looked like blood (*corn syrup*, he told himself, *food coloring*). The engine rumbled, sounding like the growl of a monster dog. A jangle like coins being rattled in a soup can came from under the hood, steam making heat waves between the cracks. There was a metal door on the side of the truck, and when it started to rise it made a creaking sound like a cemetery gate in an old horror movie. Tommy flinched. The window came up slowly, being one of those old windows that had to be hand cranked, creating a small awning over the opening.

Tommy swallowed hard. He couldn't back down now—not with everyone watching—but he suddenly wanted to. His fight-or-flight instinct was kicking in, and his entire body had voted on the latter. But he held firm, frozen by equal parts determination and stubbornness.

There was no glass barrier on the sill and the opening in the side of the truck was pitch black. He could see the edge of a counter, but beyond that there was only complete darkness, a deep, cold void. "Turkey in the Straw" blared in all its repetitious wretchedness, but there were no other noises coming from inside.

Initially, Tommy refrained from stepping up to the counter. Instead he looked at the panels on the outer wall. It was decorated like the inside of an old, yellowed comic book, with small advertisements for the goodies one could purchase; but where there should have been ice cream sandwiches, orange Creamsicles, fudge bars, and Pop Ups, instead there were promises of incredible powers and abilities, of dreams come true and wishes granted.

There was a cartoon of a muscular boy lifting a car over his head. The text read: *Be the strongest kid in school!* Another image portrayed a little girl with bright curls and brighter teeth. The text proclaimed: *Be the prettiest girl in the neighborhood!* There were many others*: Be the most popular; be the fastest; be the best football player; be the best magician; be the best dancer.* There were ads promising to make you thinner, taller, or clearer of complexion. Others gave you chest hair or a different hair color. But the one that most appealed to Tommy was an image of a smiling boy being kissed on the cheek by a pretty redhead. The text for this one was simple, yet said it all.

Get the girl!

The shadow of the truck fell over Tommy as he stepped up to the counter, his fear having given way to intrigue. Being afraid of this urban legend may have seemed stupid to him, but somehow he wanted to believe in the truck's miracles. Everyone likes to daydream about having special powers and easy fixes to their problems. Everyone wants to win that magic lottery. Tommy was no different, and when presented with such a wide array of guaranteed dreams, he allowed himself to be drawn further in by the truck's gravitational pull. He could only wonder what the cost of such granted wishes may cost, as there were no prices listed on the marquee. He was too afraid to lean in past the counter, so he just stood there, gripping it.

"Hello?" he said.

His voice echoed as if he'd called into an underground cave. There was no reply, only the terrible, empty blackness. Tommy licked his lips and looked at the picture again, its promise filling him with a luminous desire.

Get the girl!

At twelve, Tommy's hormones were in a volcanic rage. His sexuality was unfurling like an inflatable life raft, opening at a breakneck pace and shooting in all directions, but all his confused lust was directed at one target. He was in love with Harmony Sagal (or at least in love to the extent that a twelve-year-old boy understands it). With her flowing, black hair and tight, ripped jeans, she fluttered across his fantasies and danced in his dreams at night. He'd fallen hard for her ever since her family moved in a year ago, but she was three years older than him—an eternity to teenagers—so she was only vaguely aware of his existence and certainly didn't pine for him the way he did for her. She wasn't interested in him in any capacity, really. But even if they had been the same age, Tommy knew she wouldn't want anything to do with him. She was a nice girl, but exceptionally pretty and popular, far out of the league of a chubby boy with no athletic ambitions and an addiction to Xbox and Twizzlers. He could never get a girl like Harmony.

Or could he?

He pointed at the *Get the Girl* ad.

"One, please," he said.

Nothing happened. Tommy was just about to shake his head at his own gullibility when a small, white card appeared out of the darkness, sliding across the ledge as if pushed by an invisible hand. Tommy started, his breath freezing in his throat as he watched the card, waiting for it to move again, for a voice to call to him from within the truck. It looked like a blank business card the color of bleached bone. When it failed to move any farther, he slowly reached out for it, ready to draw his hand away at any sudden movements from behind the counter.

Tommy snatched it.

He bounced backward and took a few steps away from the truck. His heart was pounding and when he looked at the card, drops of his sweat fell onto it. He had expected it to say something lame like *your wish is granted*. Instead it was totally blank and—

His nail scratched along the middle of the card and a triangular flap came open, like the envelope of a greeting card. He reached in and pinched the even smaller, white card inside and brought it out. There were only two words on it, but they chilled him to his very soul.

The truck heaved forward and Tommy nearly screamed but it got caught in his chest, coming out as a squeak. The tires rolled and the great, ashen tank of the ice cream truck thundered forward, leaving Tommy in the wake of its sweet-smelling, black mist.

He heard voices.

One was Lily crying his name. The other was Mrs. Weinberg. He could see her in her second-floor window, her round face like a horrible jack-o-lantern. She seemed to be having a conniption fit. Neither of these voices mattered to him right now. The only voice he cared about came from the beautiful girl who had come running out of her house the moment the truck rounded the corner and went out of sight.

"That was incredible!" Harmony said.

She stepped in front of him, eyelashes batting, cheeks like ripe fruit. There was something different in her posture, and she was looking at him face to face, smiling at close range. He could hardly believe it.

"I never knew you were so brave, Tommy. I didn't think anyone would *ever* approach the truck!"

He tried to keep the tremble out of his voice. "No sweat."

She tucked a lock of midnight hair behind her ear, revealing rows of earrings. Her eyes were twinkling jade and there was something new in them, something he liked very much.

"You know," Harmony said. "We should get to know each other better."

•••

Nori couldn't believe her son had done something so stupid.

Hadn't she told him a thousand times about the ice cream truck?

Not that it mattered what she said to him. He was so insolent these days, so reticent with her, his puberty turning him into an arrogant lump that seemed to live solely to test her. But this was a new level of disobedience. This wasn't like failing to unload the dishwasher or leaving wet towels on the bathroom floor. What he'd done wasn't just breaking the rules; it was downright dangerous. And not just for Tommy, but for the whole family.

Nori trembled, dying for a cigarette, but she wouldn't smoke around the kids. Not around anyone, in fact. It was her dirty secret she'd gone back to her old habit after Brad ran out on her with his coworker. She'd thought their marriage was mature enough to be a trusting one. Now she kicked herself for thinking there was nothing wrong with him playing racquetball with the twenty-nine-year-old blonde. Nori felt she'd been stupid in more ways than that, though. For months, Brad had made it clear to her his bedroom needs weren't being met. She'd just been so bogged down with the store ever since she'd gotten the promotion to the middle management position. She was working long hours and coming home to two kids as well as a husband. Not to mention the damn cat! There was only so much of her to go around. Even now she was struggling with her job's demands, particularly the hours. As middle management, she was now expected to do evening and closing shifts as well as openings, a new policy had been initiated *after* she'd already taken the position. Her old eight-till-four schedule was a thing of the past, and now that she was a *single* mom, this created a whole new slew of problems.

She'd thought Tommy was responsible enough to take care of Lily and himself, but now that he'd done this, she knew she'd made a grievous error, one she might not be able to rectify that easily. Nori held her temples in frustration, not pitying herself, but cursing herself. Summer was coming, but she hadn't expected the truck to arrive so soon. No one had. The whole neighborhood was in an uproar about it, and far too many people knew Tommy had gone up to the truck—*all the way to the goddamned counter*! And the worst part was Tommy seemed to have no grasp on how serious the situation was. There was a weird, spacey look in his eyes, but no regrets.

Not yet.

"Why did you do it?" she asked him.

They were sitting at the dining room table. Lily had been sent to her room so they could talk in private (Nori had given her some cookies, proud of her for calling her at work so she could rush home). Of course, by the time she got into their neighborhood the ice cream truck was long gone, just as it always was when police cars came looking for it. But she had to get home to the kids either way. Given the extreme circumstances, no one at work had questioned her leaving early, and on her way out there was even talk of closing the store so everyone could go home to protect their kids.

"I dunno why I did it," Tommy said.

Nori sighed. "You don't *know*?"

"Yeah, I dunno. Lily was being all crazy about it. I guess I just wanted to, like, show her it was a bunch of bull."

"It is *not* a bunch of bull!" Nori hit the table with the palm of her hand and a stray pen rolled over the edge. "We've been over this again and again! Your father and I have driven it into you and you sister's heads since you were babies—*stay away from that goddamn truck*!"

"Come on, Mom. I'm not a little kid anymore."

"You're young enough. For what that truck wants, you're plenty young enough. Believe me."

Tommy pouted and crossed his arms. "This is just another fairy tale and you know it. Just like Santa and—"

"This isn't like Santa Claus!" she interrupted. She caught herself, lowering her voice so Lily wouldn't hear. "This isn't a game,

Tommy. That truck is selling something you really don't want."

His eyes darted away and Nori caught the small curl of a smile in the corner of his mouth. Her chest turned white hot. If she weren't a modern mother, she would have slapped him.

"Did you . . ."

She couldn't even bring herself to ask. It was too close to it being real.

Not again, she thought. *Not to* my child *this time!*

Tommy looked at her, his smile fading when he saw the tears in her eyes.

"Mom . . ."

Nori sat up straight. "What did you ask for?" Her son's face turned the color of strawberries. He picked at his cuticles. "Whatever it was, Tommy, it isn't worth the price."

"But I haven't—"

He stopped short, hiding something.

"You haven't *done anything* yet? Is that what you were going to say? Because that's how it works, honey. You get what you want immediately, but then you have to pay the price within a few days or weeks, depending on what the truck wants. Otherwise, everything backfires on you in the worst way, and you're far worse off than when you started."

"Come on, Mom."

"Listen to me! I've never been more serious than I am right now, you understand? You can't have things just handed to you, honey. You're supposed to work hard for the things you want and need. When someone—or *something*—just gives them to you, there's always a terrible cost. You'll wish you'd worked for the things you have once it's time to pay the bill, believe me."

Silence fell between them and she was glad to see a quiver of fear in her son's face. He damned well better be afraid. Fear might be the only thing that could save him.

"How do you know all this?" Tommy asked.

Nori hung her head, wishing she could tell him.

•••

Lily lay on her bed, petting Bibbo. The milk and cookies had calmed her down, and she was feeling a little sleepy, but remembering how strange Tommy had looked when he'd gone to the truck's counter made it hard for her to nap. It all seemed so weird, and she'd been so very afraid. Heck, she still was. Even after the truck had driven away, everything remained surrealistic to her, though she could not articulate it. Tommy had stood there in the smoke, and then Harmony, *the prettiest girl on the block*, came running out of her house to suddenly gush over him. That might have been the weirdest part of all!

Bibbo purred, making Lily feel much better.

"I love you, kitty," she whispered in the cat's ear.

Bibbo purred again in reply.

•••

That night, Tommy sat up in bed, flipping the card in his hand, half expecting what was written on it to change. His mother had demanded to see the card (Tommy wasn't sure how she knew he had one), so he fibbed and told her there'd been one on the counter but he hadn't picked it up. She could always see right through his lies. She hadn't believed him, and now he was grounded for six whole weeks, a new record by a large margin. Worse yet, she'd changed the Wi-Fi password and unplugged the Xbox and put it into her room. Mom told him she would trade him the card for the video games, but thinking of Harmony, Tommy stuck to his lie. His mother sternly warned him not to do whatever it was the card instructed, that whatever he got in return was not worth the terrible cost, but . . .

Tommy frowned at the card.

He really didn't want to pay this price, but he couldn't give up on Harmony now. She had given him more attention that afternoon than in all the time she'd lived on their street. She had even asked him to go to the movies with her—an actual *date*! Tommy didn't give a crap if he was grounded. He'd go when Mom was at work or sneak out if he had to. Harmony was a girl worth getting in trouble over. And hell, maybe things could work out without him having to do what the stupid card said. He really hoped so. But he would do just about anything to be with Harmony Sagal.

The words on the card glistened as if the ink were still wet, two words in elegant cursive.

Kill Bibbo.

•••

The next morning, Nori debated calling out from work that night, even though it was inventory time. She needed to address the situation with Tommy, but at the same time feared staying home would just draw more attention to them. Everyone on Harper Lee Dr. had seen Tommy approach the truck. All eyes would be on him now; everyone in Crestwood would be suspicious. In a small town these sorts of things traveled at light speed.

After brushing her teeth, Nori looked into the mirror, not liking what stared back at her. At forty-two, she was still extremely beautiful. People often commented she looked at least ten years younger than she was, comparing her to ageless actresses like Nicole Kidman and Julianne Moore.

You'd damn well better be beautiful, she thought, *after the price you paid.*

She shivered; first with the old, familiar self-disgust, then with a crawling dread of what was to come for her son if she didn't find a way to stop it. Staring at her reflection, Nori flashed upon the summer of 1987, back when she'd been her son's age and she'd heard the chimes of "Turkey in the Straw" in the distance. She and some of the other kids on her block had been playing at the edge of the woods where the neighborhood ended. The dead-end street was bare of houses, Crestwood being smaller then, rural. Her sister, Rita, shrieked at the sound and ran toward home, as did the other kids. This was the second time that summer the truck had come through their neighborhood, causing mass hysteria. It was the day before Labor Day, summer's farewell, and the truck was making its final rounds, offering one last temptation for the curious children of Crestwood.

While nervous, Nori had always been an inquisitive girl. She loved to learn and explore, even when doing so was dangerous. She wouldn't think twice about stepping into dark caverns filled with bats or climbing the highest trees even when the branches grew brittle. She knew she was supposed to flee from the truck, that the sound of that horrible music was like a fire alarm, but as she'd grown older the fear had yielded to the power of her curiosity, mostly because of what had happened to Derek Franklin.

The story was he had approached the truck during one Fourth of July weekend. Derek loved baseball, but was one of the worst players in the league. After the Fourth, he hit nothing but homeruns and threw pitches so fast they were merely a blur. He was only fourteen and already there was serious talk of him going pro. That all changed a few weeks later when, one night, Derek waited in the bushes for his teammate, Stephen Hodder, and bashed his kneecaps with a baseball bat, crying and apologizing to him even as he broke both of Hodder's legs. After Stephen's parents called the police, Derek confessed, saying he had to hurt Stephen if he was going to stay good at baseball, that the truck

147

demanded it. Stephen would walk again, but Derek was so distraught over what he'd done that instead of juvenile hall he went into a psych ward. That was the last anyone had heard of Derek Franklin.

Had the truck really made him good at baseball?

Young Nori couldn't help but wonder as she stood there, listening to the screeching music, hearing the rumble of the struggling engine. The truck was getting closer. The streets had cleared and even the lush, green leaves of summer's end seemed to change before her very eyes, their chlorophyll draining at the truck's steady approach. Yellow splinters crept up the leaves' spines and the kiss of decay bristled at their edges. Still the breeze blew hot like a desert storm. Nori straightened her bunched-up dress. She was overweight, and the heat had left sweat stains in every fold and divot of her flesh. She could feel the grease sizzling in her inflamed acne.

Can it really grant wishes?

She thought about poor Stephen Hodder having to use a wheelchair for months, and how he still wore a metal bracket on one knee. Nori didn't want to hurt anybody. Maybe there was a way she could get around it.

When the truck pulled up to where she stood, the peach fuzz on her arms raised and she felt sudden electricity in the air. The window shutter came up, creaking, and the dark hole behind it seemed endless, as if the arctic void led to a separate universe. She was afraid, but awed. Entering the shade the truck cast, Nori was better able to see the animated menu. Every wish a kid could have was listed on rotting stickers, but Nori had known what she wanted before she'd even stepped up to the counter. She pointed to the picture of the girl with the tiara and rosy cheeks with stars floating around her.

Be the prettiest girl in the neighborhood!

"One, please," she said.

That's when the card appeared like a spark. It wasn't until she'd come home and went up to her room she realized it was actually a small envelope. She'd been alone when the truck came, so when Rita asked her where she'd gone Nori lied and said she'd run into the woods to hide. Because of the dead-end, nobody had seen her with the truck. This was her little secret, the first of many she would keep throughout her life. And when she drew the card and read it, she was glad no one else knew about it. Derek Franklin wasn't the only one who'd been given nefarious instruction. But he had gotten good at baseball *before* he'd attacked Stephen Hodder. It was like he'd been given a bill after the fact, like paying at a restaurant. Nori went to her vanity mirror.

I'm as fat as ever.

She sighed as she turned around, looking at the lard of her butt and her tree trunk thighs. She had a pot belly and a second chin, and—

Nori looked closer.

There had been some massive, oozing zits on her chin just hours ago. Now the skin was as fresh and smooth as porcelain. She turned the desk lamp toward her face and gasped. Her complexion was completely clear, the soft ivory of a china doll. And while she still looked like herself, there were subtle enhancements to her face. Her dimples were gone and her eyebrows were arched. The small moles at the base of her neck had disappeared, and her hair had the natural waves she'd always wanted it to. Its dirty blonde was even fading back to the full blonde it had been when she was little. Tears welled in her now striking blue eyes, and when she wiped them away she felt the difference in her hand as it pressed against her cheek. Drawing it back, she realized it was no longer the swelled mitten of flesh it had been before. It was elegant, almost slender.

I'm changing.

She squealed and jumped up and down. While she was still heavy, she was transforming. It made sense for it to happen this way. If she changed too suddenly, it would draw questions, especially after the arrival of the ice cream truck. But if she gradually changed over the course of weeks, people would congratulate her on her transformation. The other girls would ask what her secret was. Would she tell them, she wondered, or keep it to herself? Let them all envy her, she decided; *let them suffer their own flaws as payback for the way they've always made fun of me.*

She squealed again.

By the time school was back in, Nori was a knockout even for her young age, dropping the jaws of everyone who looked her way, be they boy or girl. Her parents were proud of her, thinking she'd stuck to her diet and it had finally paid off. Six different boys asked her out on the first day of school, and two of them fought over her the day after that. A few weeks later she was the most popular girl in her grade. The world had opened its arms to embrace her, and she swam in the bliss of her new life, but then, just as she'd grown accustomed to her new and improved self, one day she opened her locker and was startled by the sight of the note from the truck resting on top of her books. She hadn't brought it with her to school. It was home in her dresser drawer, beneath a pile of new clothes her parents had bought to fit her new body. The card could have been some sort of prank, but Nori knew it wasn't. It was time to pay the bill. She gulped and closed the locker slowly, even though she wanted to slam it.

That night, she made the bombs.

They were crude Molotov cocktails, made out of glass pop bottles she filled with crushed styrofoam cups, gasoline, and motor oil she'd taken from the garage. She used rags as wicks and soused them in rubbing alcohol, then took the charcoal lighter from the grill. She put everything into her backpack and rode her bike to school extra early the next morning, as the card had instructed, as the card had *demanded*.

She couldn't go back to being ugly. She couldn't go from this heaven back to hell.

Going around the rear of the school to the science lab, Nori broke the windows with a rock, then lit and tossed the flaming bottles one by one, watching as the fire spread. As soon as she'd thrown the last of them, she peeled out of the lot and didn't hear the first scream until she was halfway around the side of the building. It was a high, piercing cry, the horror of which would haunt her from that day forward.

She'd thought the school would be empty this early in the morning. The card had told her to set fire to the science lab. Nori thought it would just be vandalism, and that no one would get hurt.

Tears welled in her eyes. She sped away.

School was canceled as the fire department put out the flames. Nori found out later the janitor had been cleaning the floors when the fire began, and he went into the science lab to extinguish it. The fire had reached the chemicals that were used in the class, causing it to spread quickly, trapping him in the room. His charred body was found stuck in the shattered window where he'd tried to escape. The fire chief confirmed it was arson, and the police department began an investigation. Nori spent the next month struggling with feelings of deep regret and fear. She wished she could undo it all, that she'd never approached that terrible truck. Being beautiful wasn't worth this. She'd killed someone, and now it was only a matter of time before she was caught.

But she never was.

The police never arrested her or anyone else. Nori wasn't even questioned about it. No one ever found out about her deal with the truck, and she never told anyone either. So her beauty hadn't faded. It never would. She remained gorgeous and reaped the benefits of her looks and popularity for decades to come. And somehow that made it worse. She had profited from the death of an innocent man. This caused her a great deal of mental anguish, filling her with existential guilt. She often wondered, if she'd known someone was inside, would she have gone through with it anyway? She liked to think she wouldn't have, but as she'd grown older she realized teenagers rarely think of the consequences of their actions, and they could be quite cruel and selfish. She'd felt guilty after the fact, but in that moment of choice would she have chosen to spare the life of a man if it meant she would be, in a sense, sacrificing her own life, the new identity she'd gained from her beauty?

Staring into her bathroom mirror, Nori wondered if she'd ever be able to answer that question honestly. Since the day of the fire she'd done everything she could to suppress the execrable memory, but it always came sneaking to the front of her thoughts at random moments, usually when good things were happening to her as a result of her looks, like when she drew the romantic attentions of a man she was interested in. The sound of the janitor's death-cries would come to her in these moments, sending jolts of self-hatred through her mind, always ruining what should be the most magical moments of her life. It was a hellish curse, an anchor that would forever hang around her neck, dragging her deeper and deeper into an abhorrent void much like the black insides of the ice cream truck.

She couldn't let her son suffer the same fate.

•••

Tommy stood over the toilet for a good twenty minutes but couldn't bring himself to tear up and flush the card. He wanted Harmony more than anything he could imagine, to hold her, kiss her, maybe even feel up her—

But Bibbo! Come on, not Bibbo!

They'd had the cat for five years, having raised him up from a yard sale kitten picked out of a cardboard box full of them. The cat was special to all of them, but it was most special to Lily. His little sister had loved Bibbo for practically her entire life. Lily was an irritating little twerp, but Tommy still loved her, and he didn't think he could bring himself to hurt her by hurting Bibbo. Above all else, that was the main thing—killing the cat. Like most teenage boys, Tommy's puberty-induced overload of hormones had given him the urge to stalk and kill, but there was a huge difference between going deer hunting with Dad and snapping the neck of the family pet. It was just plain wrong.

But what about Harmony?

Hell, he already had her in the palm of his hand. Maybe he could cheat somehow, get around the toll he was supposed to pay, if he was going to believe in all this hocus-pocus (which he was beginning to, all things considered). He could take Harmony out on a few dates, before the magic wore off, and show her just how much he cared about her. Then she would love him with or without the truck's help.

Tommy frowned and shook his head.

Yeah, right, tell me another one.

When the spell faded she'd take one look at his bitch tits and overbite, and she'd probably puke on the sidewalk when she realized she was holding his hand. Whatever strange power he'd purchased, he would need it to keep her interested, at least until he could figure out a way to make her love him for real.

But he couldn't kill Bibbo, could he?

Let's just take things one step at a time.

Tommy lifted the lid of the toilet tank and wedged the card between the gaps in the pump's workings, above the water. He put the lid back in place, hoping he picked a good enough hiding space, and left the bathroom. When he got back to his room, his mom was tearing the place apart. His clothes were strewn all over, his closet and dresser drawers flung open in a fury. Comic books spread out in fans across the floor, clothes sat in heaps, and his mattress was lifted and braced sideways against the wall.

Tommy's face crinkled. "What the hell, Mom?"

"Tell me where it is." She didn't even turn to face him when she spoke. "Tell me where it is or I'll rip this whole fucking room apart!"

He'd never seen Mom this furious. Unlike Dad, she rarely ever cursed. Sweat sprinkled her brow, her face flushed to a sizzling scarlet. She hadn't brushed her hair or put on makeup, and judging by the bags under her eyes, she hadn't done much sleeping. Tommy thought she looked like a raving bag lady, only prettier, of course.

"I don't have it, Mom. I swear I never even took it."

She spun around. "You're lying to me."

"I'm not, honest—"

He flinched as she charged him. Tommy stumbled into the wall. She grabbed him by his upper arms and shook him, screaming like a mad woman, making him quiver and twitch. She'd never been physical with him. His mother seemed almost alien now.

"You're lying to me, Tommy! It's written all over your face. Now tell me where it is before I smack the ever-loving shit out of you!"

Tommy was almost as tall as his mother, and certainly weighed more, so she was not physically imposing. But that didn't make him any less intimidated. She was still the mom, the authority figure, and she was *seriously* pissed. Though she'd never raised a hand to him before, not even to spank him as a little boy, he could tell by the burning behind her eyes she was just a hair away from doing so. He tried to speak but couldn't. His fear of lying to her again had turned him into a mute. Mom bared her teeth in a terrible grimace, pushed him back against the wall, and returned to ravaging his room as if she were a tornado.

Tommy cursed her under his breath. His fear turned to anger—angry with himself for being afraid of her, angry with her for still being able to intimidate him and for always trying to rule his life.

Well, he would show her, all right. She wasn't going to tell him what to do this time.

No freakin' way.

•••

"Bibbo!" Lily called into the night wind.

It was cool for this time of year and the fireflies were out, adding magic to the woods behind her house that only slightly diminished their spookiness. She had the flashlight to keep any potential monsters at bay. Lily knew she wasn't supposed to believe in them, but she wasn't sure what she believed anymore. Tommy told her one thing, Mom told her something else, Aunt Rita had her own variations, and the kids at school all had different opinions of their own. It got so Lily had trouble forming her own opinions about what was real and what was fantasy. So far, she'd decided if all of the magic she believed in turned out to be make believe, then the real world was a very sad and boring place indeed, filled only with math classes, dentist visits, moms who worked too much, and daddies who ran away from home. Lily wanted pumpkin carriages, fairies, and flying reindeer, even if they did come with scary ice cream trucks. At this point in her childhood, she needed fairy tales, just like she needed her fuzzy tabby.

"Bibbo! Where are you?"

Lily was starting to worry. Her kitty was usually back by now, knowing that sundown meant a yummy can of stinky tuna.

"I'm sure he just got carried away exploring," Aunt Rita said.

Rita was babysitting because Mom had inventory at the store and wouldn't be back until well after midnight. Lily loved her aunt. She was a plump woman with frizzy black hair who always smelled of lavender and snuck her bits of peppermint candy from time to time (their little secret). Her husband, Lily's Uncle Ralph, traveled a lot on business, and they had never had children of their own, so Rita loved to spend time with her and even Tommy (though Lily felt like Tommy was becoming a crummier brat every day).

"Bibbo *always* comes home at dinnertime," Lily said. "What if something's happened to him?"

Rita smiled her warm smile. "Let's not get carried away, Lily Bug. Cats love the night and the woods. It's in their blood to seek out adventure."

Lily knew her aunt was right, but somehow it just didn't make her any less worried.

"Tell you what," Rita said, "why don't we eat our own dinner while it's still hot, and if he doesn't come back by the time we're finished we can go look for him, 'kay?"

Lily brightened and took Rita's hand. Auntie always knew how to make her feel good when she was blue. They went through the sliding glass door and into the kitchen, and Lily set the table while Rita brought the steaming dishes from the stovetop.

"Lily Bug, go get your brother for me, 'kay?"

"Okay."

She ran down the hall and Rita warned her to slow down. She got to the door to Tommy's room, which was covered by a scary poster of a game called *Resident Evil*. Lily hated it and wished

Mom would make him take it down. Sneering, she knocked on the blood-spattered face of a zombie.

"Tommy, dinner!"

Her brother didn't reply. She didn't even hear any scuffling. Lily turned toward the bathroom. The door was wide open, the room dark, unoccupied. She knocked on his bedroom door again and called for him, louder this time. He'd be really mad if she walked right in, so she turned the knob and opened the door just a crack. The lamp by his bed was on, but the room was otherwise dark and totally still except for the curtains, which fluttered in the breeze coming through his open window.

"Tommy, Auntie wants you for dinner . . ."

Inch by inch the door came open and she poked her head inside. The room was empty.

•••

Harmony met him at the movie plaza, right outside the Quizno's. She looked stunning, ethereal, as if she herself had walked out of a movie. He'd tried to dress as cool as he could, but now he felt dopey in his short pants and *Call of Duty* t-shirt, especially seeing how dolled up she was in her blue dress and freshly styled hair.

"You look incredible," he said, his eyes as wide as his agape mouth.

She'd been smiling as she approached, but now her nose crinkled while she looked him up and down. It was a judging look, one that said she clearly didn't like what she was seeing.

"What is it?" he asked.

"Nothing, um, it's just . . . I just thought you'd look . . . *different.*"

Tommy swallowed a huge lump in his throat. "Sorry, I guess I wasn't sure what to wear."

Harmony crossed her arms in front of her. "Yeah, um, did you gain some weight?"

The lump he'd swallowed rose up again, drier, bigger. His palms grew clammy and he tucked them under his armpits. How could he have gained weight since yesterday? Why did she look so disappointed to see him?

Because you didn't do it right, he suddenly thought.

"I dunno," he said and tried to change the subject. "Are you excited to see the movie?"

"Yeah, um . . ." Harmony scratched behind her ear and looked at the pavement. "Maybe tonight isn't the best night."

Tommy's heart sank into his stomach, boiled in the acid. He'd snuck out to meet her tonight, and she'd been so enthusiastic over the phone, telling him how she hadn't stopped thinking about him since they'd last talked. Now she looked more uncomfortable around him than ever before. She'd never shown any interest in him prior to the day of the truck, but she'd always been polite, even friendly at times. Now she seemed baffled to be standing there with him, even a little disgusted.

Tommy thought of what his mom had said.

You get what you want immediately, but then you have to pay the price in a few days or weeks. Otherwise, everything backfires on you in the worst way, and you're worse off than when you started.

He'd grown so nervous before their date. All his hopes of making Harmony love him for who he was had fled in an instant. His negative self-image came swooping in like opportunistic predators. This was their first date; he couldn't afford to blow it. That's why he had done what he'd done, despite how wretched it had made him feel.

But you didn't do it right, Tommy. You freakin' blew it.

"Just give me a chance," he told her, not caring if he was begging. "Please. I mean, we're already here and you're already dressed up."

"I dunno, Tommy. Maybe this was a bad idea, you know? I mean, you're really just a kid—"

Tommy cringed.

She called you a kid. And let's face it—that's what you are. A man would've had the balls to do whatever it takes to get a girl like Harmony. But when it came time to pay the price, you just stood there in the woods like an idiot, holding the knife and holding Bibbo, not able to go through with it. The damned cat must've sensed what was going on too, because it went into a fit and ran off. Damn it, Tommy—you blew your one big chance.

Harmony was still talking.

"—I don't mean to be mean, Tommy, but let's just pretend this didn't happen, okay? I would really appreciate it if you didn't tell people about any of this."

•••

Nori did another loop through the neighborhood, shining the flashlight into the woods and between the houses, batting away her tears as she searched for her son. Her knuckles ran white on the steering wheel, nervous breaths bursting from her chest. She should have known Tommy would sneak out, even with Rita there to watch him. The boy was so damned bad these days, irremediably defiant and sneaky. She'd almost enjoyed the fear in his eyes when she'd ransacked the room and pushed him against the wall. If she couldn't have respect, maybe fear was the next best thing.

But now she was the one dealing with fear. It made her hands clammy and tightened her shoulders. When Rita had called her, she knew what had happened before her sister could even tell her. Tommy was gone, off to do some terrible deed in exchange for some big dream of his. She should have told him the truth about what had happened to her with the ice cream truck thirty years ago, but she just couldn't bring herself to do so. How could she let her child know she'd killed a man for beauty? It was so shallow and heartless, even if it had been accidental. She was so ashamed of it, and that shame was something she had locked up deep inside the vault of her soul. She hadn't even told her husband, Brad, hadn't even told her sister, Rita, who was also her best friend. How on earth could she tell her son?

In her rush she'd left work without even saying anything to anyone. Inventory was an important night—that's why she'd gone in, in spite of everything—but now it simply didn't matter. Nothing mattered except saving Tommy from himself.

Rita took her own car in search of her nephew, and Lily asked to go with her. She was concerned for Bibbo, who apparently had gone missing too, and Nori had snapped at her, telling her there were more important things to worry about, they had to find her big brother. Lily had sulked as she'd climbed into Rita's sedan. They headed into town in their separate cars, driving by all the popular hangouts for Crestwood's teens—the park, the movie plaza, the bowling alley with the black lights and glowing balls. Anything else was too far for Tommy to have ridden his bike to.

"Tommy!" Nori called into the darkness of the streets, her voice bouncing back at her from off the houses. "Tommy!"

The streets were not just dark. They were desolate. Only the bugs were out tonight, buzzing under the streetlamps in psychotic swarms. She had all her windows down, but heard nothing, not even the distant roar of the highway or the chorus of crickets in the surrounding woods. The night was huge and empty and without stars, a full dark that hid her child from her in its enveloping stranglehold.

Coming to a stop at the dead end of the street, she left her headlights on and got out of the car. She walked to the edge of the woods where the creek lay. It was Lily's favorite place to play, and it seemed like only yesterday Tommy had played with his Ninja Turtles there too. Nori would have given anything to have those days back, anything at all.

"Tommy!"

She scanned the tree line with the flashlight, gasping at every shadow, praying it was her boy. The leaves above her were rustling, crackling like wrapping paper being torn from a gift. They created static in the air. A smell of something sweet and sugary filled her nostrils, and Nori blinked away a tear as she heard the first notes chime.

Instinctively, she pushed her elbows to her sides and crouched, making herself smaller, like an animal trying to hide. Carried by the night wind, the sound of "Turkey in the Straw" drifted down the road, and when she dared to look behind her she could see a candy-colored glow coming from beyond the curve. She hugged herself but didn't go to her car. She couldn't run from this any longer, especially now that the life of her child hung in the air. With every hellish note of the song, Nori flinched and took another step away from the thicket, walking down the street, terrified but determined. The Christmas-like lights appeared at the end of the road, illuminating the eroding, pallid carrion of the massive truck. It was even more of a monstrosity than she remembered, a tower of twisted steel and scarred junk that jangled and smoked, its ugliness exasperated by the cheerful holiday glow. It moved as slowly as ever, but was drawing ever closer. Her legs threatened to give out beneath her, but she pressed on, ready to face the horror that had returned.

She stepped onto the sidewalk just as the truck came to a stop. There was a screech of grinding rust as the window came up, revealing a blackness within that was somehow blacker than the starless night. It was the most tenebrous darkness she had ever seen, an absence of light and color that seemed almost impossible. The counter was warped and dented, silently calling her forward. Nori looked all around, seeing nothing but darkened houses, all the porch lights having been turned off at the approach of the truck. At least it was too dark now for anyone to be able to see her and what she was about to do, but not so dark she couldn't see the menu. All of the old favorites were there, the very same ones that had been on the door in her childhood. She wondered which one

Tommy had selected. He was overweight, just as she had been at his age. He was unpopular, bad at sports, a mediocre student, and didn't have many friends. Just about any of the selections would have appealed to him.

But the selection didn't matter. What mattered was what price. She felt certain he'd snuck out tonight to commit whatever vile request the truck had made. She hoped she wasn't too late.

"Let him go," she said to the void.

Its only answer was "Turkey in the Straw" on an endless loop. There had to be something she could do. It was no coincidence the truck had come to her tonight. Just like before, the truck had selected her, and whether she could admit it or not, she had invited it.

Nori put her hands on the counter, hoping for instruction, but none came. She glanced back at the menu, wondering if she could find some kind of solution there, but it was just the same old cartoons and promises.

Be the strongest kid in school! Be the prettiest girl in the neighborhood! Be the most popular; be the fastest; be the best football player; be the best magician; be the best—

Then she saw it.

There was a picture of a blonde woman crouching between two smiling children, one a tall boy, the other a little girl. Above the image, bold text made the sale.

Save your kids!

Nori didn't hesitate. She pointed to her selection and gripped the counter.

"One, please, you son of a bitch."

The card appeared in a white flash and she snatched it up, afraid to look inside because she knew she would pay whatever the cost, no matter how high or horrible, if it meant Tommy would get out of paying his tab and Lily would be spared from the temptation that had lured her mother and brother.

As Nori peeled open the envelope, the truck started up. It made a U-turn as she shone the flashlight on the card inside, and as it rounded the corner she fell to her knees in shock. The truck chimed its same old song, making its same old promises to deliver the goods and damn well collect the bill.

•••

When Nori came back to the house, everyone was home, even Bibbo.

159

Rita was reaming Tommy out for sneaking away, and he was red-eyed from crying. Lily was nuzzling the cat on the sofa. When they saw Nori come in they all fell silent, and Nori went straight to Tommy and hugged him. He was surprised, probably having expected a smack to the back of the head instead of being lovingly scooped up in his mother's arms. She felt sorrow and relief coming off him.

"I'm sorry, Mom," he said. "I shouldn't have snuck out and scared everybody."

And she knew then it was all he had to be sorry for. The truck had come to her with a proposal. That meant it wasn't too late. Tommy hadn't paid his bill, not yet. Nori planned to keep it that way. She had to. Sometimes a mother has to make sacrifices for her children, painful as those sacrifices may be.

She kissed her son's forehead, told him he was grounded for two additional weeks, and sent him off to his room. It was well past Lily's bedtime, so Nori sent her off to brush her teeth, assuring her Bibbo could sleep with her tonight. Once the children were all settled in their rooms, she and Rita went out to the patio and Nori lit up a cigarette. Somehow her sister finding out she was smoking again wasn't as big of a concern as it had been before. Soon she would have much bigger things to hide from everyone.

Rita gave her a look, but didn't mention the cigarette. "He's just going through a rebellious phase. It'll pass."

"I know."

"Sorry. I should've been keeping a closer eye on him."

"Stop it, Rita. You do a great job with them. You're a wonderful sister and a wonderful aunt."

She took Rita's hand in hers and ran her thumb along the back of it. Rita pumped her hand twice when she saw Nori's tears.

"Hey," Rita said, "it's okay. Everybody's safe and sound, even the stupid cat!"

Rita chuckled and Nori forced a smile. She'd always loved her sister's laugh. It was so filled with joy, so bursting with life.

"You know," Nori said, "I could use a vacation."

"You and me both, girl."

"I was hoping you'd say that. We used to love going hiking. Let's get a cabin up at Chimney Stone, just for a night. You know, we never did make it to Potter's Cliff. I think it's high time we went right up to the edge."

Rita nodded. "You know what? You're right. It's been way too long, and we've always talked about hiking to the cliff, and we're not getting any younger. Better to do it now, while we still have the knees for it!"

Rita laughed her big, beautiful laugh again.

Nori would miss that most of all.

Thanks to CV Hunt and Andresen Prunty—goddamn, I love working with you freaks.

Thanks to Brian Keene and Mary Sangiovanni, John Wayne Comunale, Bryan Smith, Tangie Silva, Ryan Harding, Bob Ford and Kelli Owen, Josh Doherty, Wrath James White, Edward Lee, Christine Morgan, Bernard DeBenedictis, Chad Stroup, Gregg Kirby, Wesley Southard and Katie Southard, Nicole Amburgey, John Boden, and Jack Ketchum.

Big thanks to Bear.

Thanks also to Randy Chandler and Cheryl Mullenax for publishing "The Solution" the first time around, and Dawn Vogel and Jeremy Zimmerman for doing the same for "Dog Years".

And special thanks to Tom Mumme—always.

Kristopher Triana is the Splatterpunk Award-winning author of *Full Brutal, Gone to See the River Man, The Long Shadows of October* and many other terrifying books. He is also the author of the crime thrillers *The Ruin Season* and *Shepherd of the Black Sheep*. His work has been published in multiple languages and has drawn praise from the likes of *Publisher's Weekly, Rue Morgue Magazine, Cemetery Dance, Scream Magazine, The Horror Fiction Review* and many more.

He lives in a cold, dark place somewhere in New England.

Other Grindhouse Press Titles

Made in the USA
Las Vegas, NV
04 August 2022

52616920R00104